DECEPTION IN DEVON

VIVIANE'S ADVENTURES MYSTERY

VIKKI WALTON

For permission requests, write to the publisher:
Attention: Permissions Coordinator
Morewellson, Ltd.
P. O. Box 49726
Colorado Springs, Colorado 80949-9726

Identifiers:
ISBN 978-1-950452-20-0 (electronic publication)
ISBN 978-1-950452-21-7 (standard edition print)
ISBN 978-1-950452-25-5 (hardcover print edition)
ISBN 978-1-950452-26-2 (large print edition)
Front cover illustration: Rebecca Ruger
Publishing/design services: Under Wraps Publishing
Editing: Under Wraps Publishing

CHAPTER ONE

Excitement grew within me as I exited the bus. It was my first trip "across the pond" to the United Kingdom as a solo traveler. I wanted to pat myself on the back. I knew women traveled solo all the time, but this was a first for my sixty-year-old self.

Viviane Masters. Woman of the world.

Retrieving the address from my purse, I looked at my notes, and with trepidation of the hills before me, slung my backpack over my shoulder. I reached for my carry-on suitcase that I'd bought for my first housesitting adventure in Mexico. Pulling up the handle, I focused on my destination. It felt a bit silly to feel so giddy about a trip most people took without a thought. My first trip to Mexico had gone well, despite a few blips on the radar and that had given me the courage to head to Europe.

My daughter, Renne, had not been happy. "Mom, what are you thinking? At least Mexico was only a few hours away. I don't think this is a good idea." Her blond curls bobbed on her head as she set out to admonish me about my fool-hardiness.

"Renne, I'm not going to someplace crazy. I'm traveling to a first world country and they speak English. I think I'll manage." I stifled a laugh. Since when had my daughter taken on the role of caregiver with me being the child who needed guidance.

"I don't know. And living in someone's home? Doesn't that seem weird to you?"

"No. It sounds great. I loved my first housesit in Mexico and I know I'll enjoy this one as well. It's like staying at a new friend's house."

"But they're not there!" She twirled her hair with her finger, a nervous habit from childhood she'd never quite outgrown.

"Even better! I'm going to be living like the lady of the manor. Look at the pictures."

I pulled out my computer and showed Renne the interior pictures as well as the photos of the pets I'd be caring for and the area where I'd be staying. "Two cats. It's going to be tough work." I laughed.

"I don't know why I even bother." She fumed and I caught a glimpse of a miniature me and how she'd be as a mother.

"Ah, come here." I gathered her up in an embrace and kissed her on top of her head. "You know I wouldn't do anything crazy."

I felt her body shaking and she sniffed, "I miss him. Still."

Tears sprung to my eyes. "I miss him too, sweetie."

I knew that many women were widowed in their fifties or even earlier, but it had been a shock when my strong and healthy husband had died while out on a motorcycle ride with friends. It had been a long and difficult period of grief that followed. I'd thought of downsizing our large house and moving to an apartment closer to my daughter. Yet it was when my friend, Cheryl, had recommended petsitting and housesitting that I felt the first break in the fog that had seemed to envelop me for the last few years. This was something I could do, and not only could do, but wanted to do. Bruce and I had often traveled and had planned to travel even more once he retired. Now he was gone, but he had left me with the means so that I didn't need to worry about money.

I'd signed up on various housesitting platforms more on a whim than expecting anything to happen. Yet, after my first sit in Mexico, I'd been hooked on housesitting for traveling the globe by my preferred slower pace. When I'd received confirmation for a sit in London, I decided to spend some time in the beautiful area of Devon before the sit began. Planes, trains, and buses had finally brought me to this small coastal town in England.

Now here I was, and another adventure awaited. I smiled and took in the scenery for a moment. This was my new philosophy—to allow myself the time to stop and enjoy the moment. In my youth, I'd been so busy with family life or getting ahead in my career, I was always rushing to the next thing. No more rushing. No more neglecting that inner voice. No more saying —tomorrow.

"More!" I shouted. Then looked around, hoping no one thought I was a crazy old woman.

You are a crazy, old woman. Why not embrace it? I snorted a chuckle. No more apologies for being my one true self.

With a burst of energy, I plodded up the steep road to the bed and breakfast which would be my home for the next week. Readjusting the light pack which now grew heavier with every trudging step, I reached the house's entrance. It clung to the cliff face, both its signage and door were painted in a bright, cheerful blue. The door opened to reveal a pretty, thin woman in her twenties.

"Oh, hello there." She opened the door open wider. "I was on my way out. Fancy that. Looks like I came to the door in the nick of time. You must be knackered."

"No. I'm Viviane—" I realized my goof at what she'd meant. "Yes, I'm tired. Thanks."

She beamed, "Let me take that for you."

I gratefully handed over my carry-on bag which she promptly took through another door into a landing area with stairs to my left going up and down with closed doors in front of me.

"I'll put this right here for now until we find out what room you'll be staying in for your visit."

"Thank you." I removed the backpack and rubbed my shoulders. I was still in good shape for having turned sixty a few months ago, but it was a relief to remove the extra weight. "Okay, if I set this down here with my bag? It has my computer in it."

She nodded, "That's fine. I'm Ivy. Let me take you downstairs to Dianne."

I followed her down a short flight of steps to a large open doorway flanked with open wooden doors. In front of the doors, two cream Labradors lifted their chins from their beds, but otherwise, remained still.

"Is it okay if I pet them?"

"Of course. You'll be their new best friend."

"I love animals." I bent down and let the yellow Labrador sniff my hand before petting him. "Hello there, fella."

"That's Milo. He's a sweetheart. Lola's his mate. Huh, Lola?"

Lola thumped her tail but remained unmoved.

I scratched Milo behind his ears before moving over to the other bed and giving attention to Lola. Their tails thumped against the plaid dog beds as I stood up. "See you later, guys."

Milo circled his bed and finally came to a resting position. Lola laid her head on her paws, soft brown eyes following me.

I raised up from my kneeling position and waved goodbye to them before Ivy showed me to a powder room tucked under the stairs. I washed my hands and she escorted me into a lovely, large space decorated in a botanical theme.

The room's primary feature included a cozy seating area with two Chesterfield sofas facing each other. On either side of a fireplace, over-stuffed chairs in a floral chintz beckoned. Other chairs were scattered around the room. Bookcases lined the walls and I instantly longed to settle into one of the chairs with a soothing cup of tea.

I took it all in and wished to linger, but Ivy beckoned me forward. "This way, Ma'am."

We walked past the living area into a sunny conservatory where an older couple sat drinking tea in cushioned wicker chairs. The woman glanced at me from over her spectacles but didn't speak. Conversely, the elderly gentleman rose to his feet at my approach. "Please. Join us." He motioned to a vacant chair as a woman I knew to be the owner approached.

"Hello. I'm Dianne. Welcome to Kingswear House. Would you like a cuppa?"

"Yes please." I sunk into a nearby cushioned chair, happy to be off my feet after what felt like days spent traveling. Dianne spoke to the young woman as she left.

"Ivy, can you take Mrs. Masters' bags to room eight, please?"

"Okay. I'll do that before I—" Ivy's distracted attention forced me to turn toward where she was looking. A handsome man had entered the room. Something passed between the pair and I gathered that they knew one another. Certainly, he was old enough to be her father—most likely in his forties. Though I know that age differences didn't seem to stop some relationships. Maybe he was just another guest staying at the inn.

"Ivy." He nodded. "Might I have a word?"

"Yes, Mr. Fielding. How may I help you?"

"My wife has a headache. Do you know

where I might obtain some aspirin? I didn't recall seeing a chemist in town."

"I'm sure that we have some. If you'll wait here—"

"I'm on my way out. Would you mind terribly taking it up to Mrs. Fielding?"

Ivy clenched her jaw, "Certainly, sir."

The air charged with electricity. What in the world was going on between those two? I realized someone was speaking and I immediately swiveled back toward the couple sitting across from me.

"I'm sorry. What did you say?"

"May I inquire if you are an American?" The woman's voice could cut glass with its formal tone.

"Yes, that obvious, huh?"

"One doesn't want to speak out of turn, does one?" She didn't wait for my response, but primly sipped her tea from her porcelain cup.

I had to clamp my lips together to stop from giggling like a young schoolgirl. People really used 'one' in their language here? I suddenly felt very much put in my place and could tell by her attitude that it wasn't all that high on her list. Standing up, I shrugged out of my jacket and rose to place it on a nearby coat rack.

Dianne returned with a mahogany tray bearing all the accoutrements for serving tea.

Feeling a bit on display as I went through the process of pouring the tea through a strainer, I added a bit of milk to my tea and picked up the saucer. Sipping from the teacup, I was well aware of being scrutinized and realizing that I'd come up 'unworthy' in the elderly woman's eyes.

"Are you on holiday?" The man I assumed to be her husband waited until I'd set the cup back in the saucer. "Yes, I'll be staying in London, but have heard wonderful things about Devon so I wanted to visit. I plan to go see Greenway. I enjoy Agatha Christie's books."

"May I introduce myself to you. I am Alfred Bancroft and this dear lady is my wife, Margaret."

"Nice to meet you. This place is awesome."

He smiled at me, but I could tell that Margaret had placed me in the 'commoner' arena with my language. "I guess I should say 'brilliant' instead of awesome."

He laughed. "I love hearing American euphemisms for words."

I sipped at my tea, aware that fatigue was encroaching. "Are you here for vacation?"

"Margaret and I come here every year at this time. That's how we met."

She eyed me over her cup. "The tourists are normally gone for the year as the weather changes."

I almost felt admonished that I'd ruined their weekend by showing up. "I guess that means I'll have more space to roam. Maybe even check out the cliff walks."

"Those walks can be dangerous alone. One would be well-advised not to go there, especially in bad weather." Margaret intoned. "I came here as a youth until my acceptance into Oxford. The beauty can be deceiving, and with the hazards along the path it can be quite treacherous.

"Um, good to know. Thanks." I sipped at the tea as a sound from behind us caused me to turn my head. Another older couple had arrived. They approached our trio and went to one of tables in the conservatory.

Margaret set down her cup and saucer. Rising, she spoke, "One must take leave so as to dress for dinner."

Dress for dinner? Yikes, I hope I had something that would be considered appropriate.

They nodded at the other couple as they passed, her husband trailing after her like a courtier in waiting.

Dianne came out of the kitchen. "Tea, Mrs. Caldwell?"

The woman set her bag on a nearby table. "We'd love a cuppa. Rodney?"

"Yes. 'Ello." He grinned at me as he walked by. "I don't believe we've met."

"I'm Viviane Masters."

He took my hand and nodded with his head. "Mrs. Masters."

"Please call me Viviane."

"Nice to make your acquaintance, Viviane. I'm Rodney Caldwell and this lovely lady is my wife, Edda. Are you here alone?"

"Rod!" his wife hissed under her breath, "You don't ask a lady that."

He faced me again. "My apologies for being cheeky. I meant if you were alone, would you care to join us at our table for dinner this evening?"

"Yes, that would be very nice. I'd like that. Thank you."

"Finished?" I looked up to see the owner staring intently at me. All the varied English accents had me grinning like a Cheshire cat. Dianne must be wondering if she had a crazy person staying at her establishment.

"Oh yes. Thank you." I handed her the cup. She set it next to the other tea items before picking up the tray.

"Cocktails are at seven. Dinner at eight. If you'll head up to the landing, Ivy will meet you and escort you to your room." She headed toward a door that I gathered led to the kitchen. I heard her call out "Walkies!" Milo and Lola jumped from their beds but headed toward the

11

upstairs landing. Maybe they weren't allowed back here.

Bidding goodbye to the Caldwells, I returned upstairs to the main floor, where my bags sat off to the side. I noticed Alfred closing a door to a room directly off the landing. He saw me and nodded.

I nodded back, wondering if that was the appropriate gesture. I hoped I could handle the more formal cultural customs and not make a fool of myself.

I waited for Ivy to return as a door opened and Alfred stepped out. "Well, hello again. Do you require any assistance?"

"No thanks. I'm waiting for Ivy to take me to my room." I pointed toward my bags.

"Very well. Forgot my book downstairs." He closed the door behind him and made his way back to the conservatory. I was about to go back down as well and find Dianne when Ivy rushed out of another doorway. I could see that it led to a back staircase, but what was more interesting was a glimpse of a male figure. What was Mr. Fielding doing in the private area? Maybe it wasn't private, but another way to access the downstairs.

Her face flushed; Ivy led me up to the next level. It was hard to think of it as the first floor, but I know that the entrance was considered the ground floor. We arrived at my door which was directly over Alfred and Margaret's room. Ivy stepped back to allow me to enter the room first which was decorated in colors of soft buttercream and pansy blue.

"Let me know if you require anything else." She shut the door behind her as I approached the window which overlooked the river. At the far point you could see the ruins of a castle battlement and beyond that the open water of the English Channel.

Glancing at the time on the bedside clock, I still had a few hours before cocktails and dinner. Pulling my clothes from my suitcase, I took my dress into the bathroom, hoping the steam from the shower would remove any of the wrinkles. If not, I'd have to break out the iron and I didn't relish that since I didn't even own an iron anymore.

After a nice, warm shower, I towel-dried my silver hair which I'd cut short for the trip. I pushed up the window, allowing the breeze to come into the room. Moving the chair to face the view, I enjoyed watching the boats travel up and down the river. However, it wasn't long before my eyes grew heavy and it was an hour later when I awoke with a start.

Wiping my eyes, I glanced over to where the clock sat on the bedside table. Noting that

I still had time before cocktails, I took my time waking up. The air had turned cooler, probably what had caused me to wake, and as I went to shut the window, I heard voices. The woman's voice I didn't recognize. I couldn't hear everything, but I could tell by her tone that she was angry. The only words I could make out were 'that girl' and 'stop being silly.' That male voice I did recognize. It was Charles Fielding. Ah, had he been doing some flirting with Ivy and it had backfired on him? That could also explain her manner towards him that I'd witnessed.

In the bathroom, I surveyed my dress. It had been a good investment as I'd purchased as many items that were purported to be wrinkle-free as possible. I shimmied into my navy dress, and accessorized it with a white, navy and gold scarf I draped over my shoulders. I had brought minimal jewelry with me, so I fastened my pearl stud earrings after applying a light application of makeup. Hopefully, I would surpass Miss Moneybags' expectations.

The sound of doors opening and closing signaled that others must be headed downstairs. I approached the standing Cheval mirror in the corner, giving myself a once-over before joining the other guests. For some reason, I felt especially self-conscious and nervous. Hopefully, I wouldn't stick out like a sore thumb. At least the Caldwells seemed nice enough.

As I entered the living room, I spied Margaret sitting in one of the two chairs next to the fireplace. A fire had been lit in the hearth and its crackling brought a warm ambience to the room. I didn't see Alfred but was happy to see another couple enter the room as I accepted a canape and napkin from Ivy, now dressed in a crisp white blouse and black skirt.

The man was frail with his wife being sturdy in comparison. The couple took a seat on one of the sofas and accepted the small bites from Ivy who was flitting from person to person. Ivy leant down and told me the couple's surname was the Carlyles. Another younger couple arrived, and I realized it must be the Fieldings.

The young woman sat down across from the couple and accepted a glass of wine. Mrs. Fielding spoke to the older woman who'd arrived ahead of them, "I'm sorry to be staring. You look so familiar to me. Have we met before?"

Mrs. Carlyle politely answered, "I don't think so, dear."

"I guess you remind me of someone." She took a sip of her wine.

While she sat on the sofa, Charles stood behind her. Dianne offered Catherine the tray, but Charles declined with a shake of his head.

He didn't acknowledge or speak to anyone so the tension between Charles and his wife must still be simmering from their earlier confrontation. What, or more likely, who had they been arguing about? Maybe it wasn't about Ivy. I got carried away thinking about them making this trip as a last ditch effort to save their marriage.

Two women arrived, one tall and one petite, stopping my musing about the couple. They greeted us all in a loud hearty welcome. From their accents I could tell they too were American, and we chatted as Ivy took our orders for drinks.

A beautiful young woman arrived, and we all turned as she announced her entrance. Mr. Carlyle struggled up from his place. "Daphne, luv, here take my seat."

"Thank you, Edmund." She looked around and spied Alfred in the chair next to the fire opposite Margaret's. "I think I'll stand by the fire. It's so inviting." She strode toward the fireplace, all eyes on her. Alfred stood, "Allow me." He waved at the seat he'd vacated.

The young woman demurred, "I couldn't. Please. I'll just stand here."

"No, please. Take my seat."

She smiled up at the elderly gentlemen and sat down in the chair which sat in center pride of place in the room. Alfred moved over to stand beside Margaret's chair. I admired his chivalry, a courtesy not seen as much in this modern day and age.

Daphne scanned the room and as her gaze landed on Catherine Fielding, an odd look came over her face. She stared at the other woman for a while before she jumped up from her spot, "Excuse me, I forgot something." Daphne rushed from the room.

Was she the woman that Catherine had spoken about? I didn't know how long either of them had been staying at the inn but there was no doubting the allure that Daphne evoked when she'd arrived in the room.

I realized that the Caldwells hadn't arrived yet. Maybe they'd gone for a pre-dinner walk instead of cocktails. After a while, I spotted Daphne returning. She appeared to have added more eye makeup. She's also put her hair up into an upswept bun. Maybe she felt she was under-dressed for the occasion. Whatever, the reason, she looked quite changed from her earlier, more natural, appearance.

The conversations were lively but reserved as more hors d'oeuvres were passed out to all the guests. I accepted an offered glass of white wine and enjoyed the feeling that I was in a proper English home with a variety of people. I scanned the crowded room over my wine goblet and smirked to myself.

The only thing missing is the murder.

I swallowed too quickly at that morbid thought and sputtered as Ivy came to my aid. "Are you okay, luv?" She handed me a napkin.

I nodded my head, realizing the other younger woman had joined her and was patting my hand. Geez, I felt old. "I'm fine. Sorry. Must have gone down the wrong pipe."

Catherine turned to her husband, "Charles, can you get her a glass of water?"

Ivy stood up. "It's okay Miss Fielding, I can do it." She strode purposefully from the room.

I felt all eyes on me as I regained my composure. So much for fitting in and not making a fool of myself.

Finally, plates and glasses were removed, and we were instructed to move into the dining area. Unsure what to do, I felt a hand on my elbow as Mr. Caldwell joined me. "Allow me." He waved toward the dining room where his wife, Edda was already seated. I sat across from them as the first course of a broth soup was presented.

I took a sip of the broth and found that I had been seated with my view directed toward the Bancrofts. I smiled, but she lowered her gaze to her soup.

Geez. That woman was a tough nut to crack.

I turned my attention to my dinner companions. "It's really beautiful here. Do you come here often?"

Rodney began, "We come every year for a few days, but this time we're here for a fortnight. When I was a young lad, I was sent down from London on the trains to get us away from the bombings."

"Wow. I'd heard of that, but never met anyone who experienced it."

He wiped his mouth with his napkin before continuing, "I recall walking along the river and a submarine came right up out of the water." He tilted his head toward the window which looked out over the river, now dark with the night. "Let me tell you, I was gobsmacked. That was an exciting moment to be sure."

"I'd be gobsmacked too. I can only imagine." I realized that I was sitting with living history.

"What are you planning on doing while you're here, dear?" Edda inquired.

"I'm simply enjoying some time walking around and seeing the sites. Tomorrow I'll be going to the Coleton Fishacre estate and the following day I'll head up to Greenway."

"Are you a mystery fan, then?"

"Yes. Mystery and history. After this I'll be traveling to London where I'll be staying for a while watching over some cats."

"That's interesting. Do you have friends there?"

"No, I'm petsitting for them. I only found out about housesitting a little while back. It's a great way to travel but stay in a nicer home environment. Plus, I love animals so it's a great win for everyone."

The soup was removed, and a fish course presented. The owner let us know that the fish had been caught that day. I tucked into the fish and side of roasted potatoes as my lunch had consisted of some snacks on the train and the cookies—what they had called biscuits—at tea had only helped to stave off the hunger for a while longer.

Rodney set his fork and knife down. "If you're interested in history, then you should visit the memorial to the Americans. It's around the point past the ruins."

"Memorial?" I wiped my mouth.

"The Americans were practicing at Slapton Sands for their D-Day attack. The beach was similar, so they were using it to learn. Unfortunately, someone shared the information with the Germans, and over seven hundred men were killed."

"Oh, that's horrible." This was some history I'd never heard of before.

"Yes it was. We had a saying back then,

'Loose lips sink ships.' Someone must have told them." His face flushed and Edda reached over and took his hand. He smiled at her and something meaningful passed between them.

He patted her hand. "Well, If it weren't for ... You Yanks saved us."

I'd never been called a Yank before and probably never would be again, but I felt a swell of patriotism for those who had given so much for others. "Thanks for telling me that story. I'll try to get over there before I leave. Can I walk to it?"

"It's pretty far past that bend. I'd say a little over eleven kilometers. You might need someone to take you. I think that you could rent a car too."

"Oh, okay. Well if not this time, it will give me an excuse to come back."

Our plates were removed to have a plate of cheese and fruit set in front of us. Dianne offered the table a glass of port, and I accepted. The warm drink soothed me, and I settled back into my chair.

"Would you mind a picture?" Rodney popped up from his chair and motioned for me to join his wife.

I was certainly used to the younger selfie crowd, but this seemed a bit different. I didn't want to refuse, so I consented.

"If you can move over to my place, I'll take a picture of you and Edda."

Setting my napkin down on the table, I exchanged places with Rodney.

He picked up his camera. "Say cheese."

I smiled at the camera as I heard the shutter click, something you didn't hear much anymore with cameras built into phones. His face was intent as he motioned for us to come closer together. He took a few pictures and looking at them said, "Yes, yes, those will do nicely."

He showed them to us and while I saw our smiling faces, it was the face behind us that glared with a look of intense animosity that caught my attention. It was Margaret Bancroft.

CHAPTER TWO

The light filtering through the window curtains woke me the next morning. I yawned loudly and stretched my arms over my head. While I'd slept hard, glimpses of a dream kept trying to force its way into my conscious mind.

I didn't remember the dream, but I did know the subject. It was Bruce. After all this time, he still came to me in my dreams, laughing or on some nights, waving goodbye as he'd done on that fateful day. I reached over and touched the empty pillow next to mine. Having lived with another person for so long, it felt as if a piece of me was missing.

Pushing back the covers, I strolled over to glance out the window. Spying the castle ruins on the point, my thoughts flew to the men who had given their lives fighting against tyranny. It had certainly seemed to upset Rodney. He couldn't have been much older than ten or twelve at the time, but I knew that looks could be deceiving. Maybe he was older. People were living well into their nineties and hundreds now. A flash of memory from the night before came to me. The picture he took of me and Edda went through my mind. It was almost as if he had positioned himself to ensure Margaret was in the picture. But why do that?

"You're letting your imagination run away with you again." The sound of something falling startled me. I grabbed my robe and rushed from my room. I was tying the ends together when I met Rodney on the landing. "Did you hear that?"

He nodded and shot down the stairs surprisingly well for his age. As we reached the landing, Dianne came through a side passage which must lead down into the kitchen. She turned toward us, "Ivy said—"

Dianne went over to the door and knocked solidly. "Mrs. Fielding, is everything all right?" She spun around to address Ivy who had now joined the group. "Ivy, go get the keys." She banged on the door again. "Mrs. Fielding!"

"What about Mr. Fielding?" I stepped forward as other guests came out of their adjoining rooms and met us on the landing.

"He went out this morning for a walk. That is why I'm concerned." Dianne knocked again. "Mrs. Fielding, are you in there?"

She turned to us. "I think it would be best if everyone returned to their rooms for now. Breakfast is being served downstairs for you. The cook is ready to take your orders."

Edda, who had come downstairs, now clutched at Rodney and he pulled her close to his side. "I'm gutted, Rod."

"Shhh. It simply proves it." They headed back up the stairs together.

Proves it? What did he mean? I turned back to see Ivy heading up from the back passage. Then it dawned on me that the Bancrofts had not left their room. "Are the Bancrofts here?"

Dianne faced me. "They're taking breakfast in the conservatory. You can find them there." It was a curt dismissal. I nodded and went back up to my room where I dressed in an outfit appropriate for the day's walk.

I was sad to see that Milo and Lola were away from their beds, maybe enjoying their breakfast as well. I entered the breakfast room, Alfred rose and beckoned for me to join him. I didn't have any desire to do so but didn't want to appear rude either.

"I thought Margaret was down here."

"She had to return to our room for a moment. She'll join us shortly."

I sat down, but my thoughts rushed back to earlier. She hadn't joined us in the hallway. Neither had the other young woman from last night. Wouldn't they have heard it? Of course, I'm nosy about everything so others may not have been as curious. But when Dianne knocked on the door it would have seemed they would have come to their doors at least. Of course, I had been focused on Dianne so maybe they had, and I just didn't notice it.

"Something puzzling you, my dear?"

I realized he had been speaking to me. I shook my head. "No. Just distracted. Sorry." I pulled the napkin from my plate and positioned it across my lap.

The cook came out from the kitchen to take my order. I decided on scrambled eggs with avocado toast. Sipping the hot coffee that she'd set down on the table was a welcome distraction from my thoughts and what could be happening upstairs.

"Did you sleep well?" Alfred inquired.

"Yes, thank you. I think the delicious meal and the port saw to that."

An uneasy silence filled the air, so I took another sip of coffee.

Finally, I came up with a suitable line of questioning. "Did you meet at Oxford?"

Alfred spoke, "Oh no, my dear. We've only recently married."

Surprise must have been evident on my face as he continued, "We met four years ago on my birthday. The year I turned ninety."

The cook came over and placed the food in front of me. After thanking her, I said, "I hope you don't mind me saying, you certainly don't look like you're in your nineties."

Margaret had appeared at the table. "One doesn't mind but prefers not to be reminded." It was a polite reprimand of Alfred, who stood and pulled out Margaret's chair.

So Margaret was also at least ninety. That would mean she would have been in her teens during the war. "Were you also sent down here during the war? Mr. Caldwell said he had been sent down here during that time."

"Only a short while during the war and then I returned to my home on Jersey."

Jersey? Why did that sound familiar? Maybe I was thinking of New Jersey, in the states.

I dug into the eggs and toast the cook had placed in front of me. "Did you see what happened to Mrs. Fielding? Is she okay?"

"Mrs. Fielding?" Margaret furrowed her brows.

"Yes, they're in the room next to yours."

"Mr. and Mrs. Caldwell are in attendance of that room."

"But—"

"One heard a commotion, but that is all. One doesn't pry into the affairs of others."

Well, she'd certainly put me in my place once again.

Alfred defused the situation by saying, "The food they do here is proper tasty."

"Yes, it is." I switched back to the topic. "Mrs. Bancroft, the Caldwells are upstairs next to my room. Mrs. Fielding may have fallen or something else fell in that room."

"One is mistaken."

I started to respond but decided against it.

"Good morning." We all turned to see the Caldwells enter. Mrs. Caldwell held a skein of yarn and as she passed our table. I couldn't help but notice the strange look on Margaret's face. What was it between these people? I knew that class distinctions even showed up in the states, but this staid repellence was something I'd never experienced. The undercurrent of emotion was palpable.

Alfred rose, "Ma'am." He nodded. "Sir." They shook hands and the Caldwells passed by to sit at another table next to the conservatory window.

"Excuse me, please. I'll be back in a minute." I wiped my mouth with my napkin and walked over to the pair.

Edda looked up and smiled. Rodney was not his normal jovial self. "Rodney, did you find out what happened to Mrs. Fielding?"

He shook his head. "They've rung for a medic. She has a nasty cut on her head from a fall."

"Oh, that's terrible. I hope she'll be okay. Well, enjoy your breakfast." I returned to our table only to have Margaret say, "Alfred and I must take our leave." Alfred rose and pulled out her chair for her. They left and their plates were cleared.

The two American women entered, chatting amicably. I invited them to join me, which they gladly accepted.

"I'm Candace and this is Holly. We didn't get to talk much last night."

"Well, glad we have a chance this morning. Are you two on vacation?"

Holly replied, "We're on holiday, yes."

"What's up with you?" Candace accepted a glass of fresh squeezed orange juice and they placed their breakfast orders.

"I'm trying to speak properly while we're here."

"Well, stop it. It makes you seem silly." She

poured coffee for her and Holly who was miffed at the dressing-down.

Candace spoke, "Don't worry about her. She always gets her panties in a knot over silly things."

"I do not." She huffed and crossed her arms.

"You do too." Candace replied, "Now, shhh. You're getting too loud."

"Oh my gosh. You're sisters!" I laughed.

"Whatever gave us away?" Candace winked.

The food arrived and we chatted about our homes, love of travel, and the incident with Mrs. Fielding.

Holly spoke, "It's terrible. Poor Charles looked as white as a ghost."

"I think he was out walking is what they said." I speared a tomato on my plate.

"Hm ... I wonder about that."

I glanced at Candace. "What makes you say that?"

"I could swear I saw him in the back stairwell area not long afterwards, so he had to have come back at some point."

"Really? Are you sure it was him?"

"No. I had come up the main stairs after talking to Dianne about our room. He was some-what hidden by the door, but there was definitely a man there. Besides, I think he was the only one wearing a light blue shirt today."

"Maybe he went out the back way for his walk."

She shrugged, "Could be."

Holly leant toward me, "They loaded her up in an ambulance and he followed after her. So he must have taken a shorter walk because he was definitely back when the medical team arrived."

"Wow, I didn't even hear any of that going on from down here."

Candace leaned in. "I'm sure this house has to be really sturdy because of where it sits, and they probably added insulation if they planned for it as a guesthouse. Much quieter that way. I know I hate traveling and the hotel walls seem like paper they're so thin." She swiveled to look at the kitchen before turning back and continuing, "Plus, they probably don't want a lot of noise. It could be bad for business I bet." She picked up a piece of my toast from the rack and smeared it with orange marmalade. Do you mind? I'm starving."

I set the rack between us. "Have at it. There's plenty and I can get more if we want it."

"While it's sad that the Fieldings are leaving, it will be good for us." Holly interjected. "It's a much bigger room and they can split the bed into two twins. That queen isn't cutting it."

Candace laughed, "Well, if you weren't such a bed-hog."

"More like if you weren't such a blanket thief." Holly stuck her tongue out.

I gazed at the pair, who appeared to be in their late sixties, as they bantered between themselves. It was evident that they loved one another, and the remarks were all in fun. It would be such a delight to have a sister like that.

I heard a sound and the woman that had arrived with the other couple walked in and stood at the door. I struggled to remember her name and came up short. Faces I could recall but names were often touch and go.

Holly grew excited and waved with her hand, "Come join us. We've got room here."

The woman approached quietly. "Thank you." She sat in the chair next to me and spoke so quietly all of us leaned in to hear her. "I'm Daphne Haywood."

"Hello, Daphne. Pleased to make your acquaintance." As Holly spoke, Candace rolled her eyes at me and I tried not to burst out laughing.

"I'm Holly and this is my sister, Candace. We're from Florida. Where are you from?"

I realized Holly's gaffe, but Daphne replied, "I reside in Buckinghamshire."

Holly grinned, "That sounds so cool. I'd love to say I lived in a shire." Then dropped her head and put her napkin over her mouth, realizing she'd resorted to her normal unreserved nature.

"Hello." Daphne looked at me and I realized that we hadn't been introduced.

"Hi. I'm Viviane." I could tell she was studying me, but in a different manor than that of Mrs. Bancroft.

"Charmed." She turned back toward Holly and spoke to her.

Candace said, "Are the Carlyles your parents?"

"No. Sadly. Jocelyn and Edmund are my guardians."

I guess she noticed the puzzled look on my face. "They were my guardians after my parents died. They're the only family I have." She lowered her head to compose herself, and we waited.

Looks passed between us, but none of us spoke the question on our minds of what happened to her parents. Instead the conversation returned to much lighter topics of shopping and fashion. I listened as the three chatted before saying, "I need to get going as Ivy is going to drop me at Coleton Fishacre."

"That's where we're going today. You can go with us." Candace responded.

"Great. Let me find Ivy to tell her, then I'll get my bag and be right down."

Holly followed Candace in getting up to leave. "Please excuse us too, Daphne. Nice chatting with you."

Daphne answered with a polite, "Goodbye." No doubt she was probably happy to be rid of three chattering females and enjoy her breakfast of eggs, and smoked kippers in peace.

I found Dianne working at a desk in an alcove by the kitchen. Milo and Lola sat close by, and their tails thumped the ground as I entered. After giving them proper greetings and pets, I let Dianne know that I would be going with the sisters to the national trust site, so Ivy didn't need to drive me. She agreed to tell Ivy for me.

I passed back through the breakfast room which was now empty and made my way up the landing. Having not wanted to lug my key around with me, I'd neglected to lock my door when I went down for breakfast. However, when I opened the door to my room, I found myself staring at Alfred. My mind tried to make sense of it, and I realized that the landings looked exactly alike. I sputtered, "I'm so sorry. I thought this was my room." I blushed at my mistake.

"Not to worry." Alfred came toward me as I stepped back out onto the landing. I did hear the click of the lock as I made my way to the stairs.

The door to the Fieldings room next to the Bancrofts stood ajar. I glanced inside to see Ivy working on pulling the bed apart. I walked into the room, "Do you need help with that?"

"No, I can get it."

"Look, I can see that it's not an easy task. Let me help."

"Thanks. I'm dividing this king into two twins for the ladies upstairs."

"This place is a bit like musical chairs, isn't it?"

She laughed, "This room definitely is. First it was the Caldwells, then the Fieldings, and now the two American ladies."

So Mrs. Bancroft had been right. I'd just assumed that the Caldwells had always been in the room next to mine. When had the Caldwells vacated the room and the Fieldings taken it? I gathered up a bedsheet, "I was sorry to hear about Mrs. Fielding. I hope she'll be okay."

Ivy set the pillows down. Her face grew red and blotchy as she struggled not to cry.

"Are you okay?" I couldn't help my natural mothering instinct and rushed over to Ivy. Taking her arm, I led her to a high-backed chair.

She gathered her composure. "I ... anyway." She took a calming breath. "I'm glad she's going to be okay. I don't know how she could have fallen and hurt herself so badly. I think she could have even died if we wouldn't have found her."

"But we did. I'm sure she'll be okay. Do you

still need my help? I'm supposed to meet the sisters and go with them to the national trust estate."

She shook her head, took a tissue from her pocket, and blew her nose. "I'll be fine. I've never had that happen in all my days."

All her days? She was probably in her early twenties.

I turned to leave when a thought came to me. "Ivy, correct me if I'm wrong, this was the Caldwell's room, but then it was the Fieldings?"

"It was. But they were only going to be staying for a few more days. I guess they decided to stay on longer and asked if they could be moved upstairs. The Fieldings would only be here for the weekend—or would have been. I don't know why the Caldwells want to do that as they now have to climb two flights of stairs from the dining room."

Our eyes met and her face flushed as she realized I'd read between the lines on her thoughts that the couple were elderly and couldn't climb many stairs. I realized that probably anyone in their forties would be considered old to her. The thought of Charles came to my mind. He had to be in his late thirties or early forties. Was Ivy "that girl," whom Catherine had been referring to in their spat?

Ivy grabbed a pillow, "Anyway this room had already been reserved for the Fieldings."

I guess that made sense. "So they switched with the Fieldings? When did that happen?"

"They must have done it while everyone was at dinner last night. When I went in to clean and change the linen, they were all packed up to move."

The Caldwells must have been changing their rooms around the time we were all having cocktails.

"One last question, Ivy. When did the Caldwells decide to stay on longer?"

She tilted her head, puzzling it out. "I think a few days before you arrived. Yes, I remember that Dianne had checked in the Bancrofts a few hours earlier."

"Wait, so if it was reserved—"

"Lucky for the ladies, the other couple cancelled." She plumped the pillow and set it on the bed.

Excusing myself, I went to my room, finding it locked. Ivy must have locked it when she cleaned my room while I was at breakfast. After getting her to unlock my door, I realized I'd need to take my key with me from now on while in the house.

I changed out of my flats and into a pair of sneakers before meeting Candace and Holly downstairs on the front landing. So the Caldwells had decided to stay on after the Bancrofts arrived. Well, after Holly and Candace changed rooms, hopefully things would settle down.

Gathering up my bag and a light jacket in case of rain, I found Holly and Candace waiting in the drawing room. "Ready?" Candace rose from her chair.

"Looking forward to it. Thanks for letting me tag along with you two. I was telling Ivy I didn't need a ride now."

Outside Candace led me over to a Mercedes. "Wow, that's a nice rental."

"It's not like us to spring for something like this normally. It wasn't any more expensive than other cars and I have no desire to drive a manual vehicle. You'd be surprised how many people own this brand in England. Not so far to ship. You can sit up front with me and Holly will take the back."

"Is that okay with you Holly? I'm more than able to sit in the back."

She grinned at me, "Not a problem. I'm shorter and the front is better for you tall ladies."

"Thanks." I started to get in on the right side before catching myself. "Old habits."

I went around and got in on the left. Candace was already behind the wheel once I was seated.

"I think it would be hard to get the hang of driving on the other side."

"A lady who lives over here told me the secret to driving anywhere different is to always keep your eye on the white or dividing line. That the right course is always 'on your shoulder facing the side window' so to speak."

"I would never have thought of that, but that's right. Though out here, from what I've seen there aren't any lines on the road."

"Yep, this will be a first for me too." She winked at me. "Adventure, right?"

I gulped and nodded as she put the car in drive, and we started on our journey. I felt some trepidation as we made our way down a small road with tall hedgerows on either side, hoping we wouldn't meet another car along the way. However, Candace was utterly focused on her task, so I settled in for the short drive.

At Coleton Fishacre, we chose to separate once we reached the house, with a plan to meet up in a few hours. I was glad for the time alone and enjoyed strolling the walled garden. Even though it was late in the season, the flowers still held their blooms, some even supplying a hint of fragrance as you walked past.

After exploring outside for a while, I made up way to the home's entrance. The house's interior signaled a by-gone genteel era and I loved exploring its many nooks and crannies. I could easily imagine a singer on the steps leading into the saloon, a name I associated with the wild west instead of a living room. I envisioned women drinking their Hanky Panky cocktails in long beaded gowns and men with slicked back hair stood next to the art deco fireplace in their tuxes. This glimpse into a bygone era was an unexpected treat.

Later after touring a bit more of the grounds, I found Candace and Holly at the café enjoying a sandwich and soup.

I joined them. "I think I'm going to walk out toward the path to the cliffs."

"If you're going to eat first, we'll go with you."

I agreed, ordering a bowl of soup and a currant scone with Devonshire cream. After finishing our lunch, we walked along the path that meandered through dense foliage. I could easily visualize a dinosaur coming forth from them, so otherworldly was the landscape.

I realized Candace was speaking to me. "Sorry? My mind was elsewhere."

"My mind wanders like that too. I was saying what do you think of the other guests? Especially the Lord and Lady?"

I immediately knew who she meant. "I think that they're of a different class and culture, and it could even be a generation-thing, but they seem to be nice people."

Holly piped up, "He does. Not so sure about her though. Something about her bothers me."

Candace snapped her fingers, "I got it. Her nose is so stuck up in the air, she'd drown if it rains."

I knew better than to say anything and tried to change the subject, but to no avail.

"What about the Caldwells?" Holly hesitated over a hilly portion of the trail and we stopped so she could catch her breath.

"I like them." I replied. "They seem very nice."

Candace nodded. "Yes. Also the other couple. What's their name, Holly?"

"The Carlyles?"

"Yes. That's them. They're the couple who are with Daphne."

I nodded. "I haven't met them yet."

"They're nice enough. But quieter and more reserved. Though, I have overheard her spatting with him. Maybe she's nice in person but mean in private. He definitely looks beat down."

Holly interjected, "Honestly, it surprised me that Daphne sat with us this morning."

A light mist held the promise of rain as we made it to the wooden gate that led to the coastal path. "I think we may need to start heading back." I shrugged into my jacket.

"Agreed." They chimed. Luckily, we made it to the car before the downpour started.

Back at the bed and breakfast, I shook off my umbrella and shucked out of my damp coat. In the entry, I pulled off my wet sneakers and left them there beside a group of wellies. It would have been nice to have a pair of those boots when my foot slipped into a large puddle. I trudged upstairs and turned on the electric kettle to make a nice hot cup of tea.

After toweling off my damp hair, I fired up the computer. An email with a familiar name jumped out at me. It was from Perry. I'd met him in Mexico while on my first house sit. We'd struck up a friendship while there, though over the months, our correspondence had been fairly lax. The message was simple.

Chat later? Eleven your time. Too late? Got News.

I replied with an affirmation, and a bit of excitement at talking to him again. What news was he going to share with me?

CHAPTER THREE

I'd been asked to join the Carlyles for dinner and spent an enjoyable evening with them and Daphne. After the dinner had been cleared, we all retired to the drawing room where a fire blazed on the grate. Alfred and Edmund took up a game of chess while Jocelyn sat reading a book. Margaret had gone up to their room while the other ladies convinced me to play a game of cards.

"Gin!" Daphne smiled. "I win again."

"You're good at this." Candace remarked.

Daphne smirked and it was my first glimpse at a different nature than one she usually presented to the world. Her look was more of pride than accomplishment. "Thank you. I am good at strategy."

"Me too." Candace remarked. "I'm pretty

competitive when it comes to games. Do you play a lot of games?"

"Sometimes." Daphne expertly shuffled the cards from one spot to another in her hands before handing them over to Holly. "I know that if I play, I always play to win. Who doesn't?"

Holly looked at the two women. "I enjoy playing. I think you both are extremely competitive."

Daphne glanced over to the woman reading, "What do you say, Jocelyn? Am I competitive?" Jocelyn looked up from her book.

She didn't answer immediately, then responded, "Lucky. And smart. You're a clever woman, luv."

Her answer seemed to satisfy Daphne, who returned her attention to where Holly was dealing the cards for the next round.

I picked up the cards and put them in order before stating, "I didn't see Rodney and Edda in the dining room tonight. Are they okay?"

Holly looked up from her hand, "I believe they must have made other dinner arrangements. I overheard Rodney telling her that they had to go somewhere this evening. So maybe a place that's only open on certain days."

We continued our game, passing the winner's baton between Candace and Daphne. It was hard to tell who was the more competitive of the two.

Excusing myself as the time grew late, I passed Dianne coming in with the dogs on their leads, their tongues hanging out with contented pleasure. After a quick hello and a pat for both Milo and Lola, I excused myself. I headed toward my room, wanting to get into something more comfortable before my chat with Perry.

A flutter in my stomach made me halt for a moment. Butterflies? At my age. Really, Viviane. Get a grip.

He's nice enough, but there's certainly no romantic inclinations from either side. He's a good friend though. I wondered if I was trying to convince myself that what I felt was simple friendship but no matter what, I knew I was glad to hear from him.

I dressed in my silk pajamas and robe. Positioning the pillows behind me, I made myself comfortable on the bed before signing into the online platform. Okay, I had added a swipe of lipstick but other than that, I hadn't done anything else. Still the more I thought about it I wondered if I should change out of my pajamas into something more presentable.

What's with you, Viv? You're acting like a kid. I have a robe on for goodness sakes. Plus, it's not like an online date or anything.

A noise from the computer let me know that he was calling in. I propped a few pillows up and checked the video before going live.

"Hello there!" Perry waved at the screen and I could see he was up on the mirador of his house. I caught a glimpse of Lake Chapala in the background.

"Hello to you too."

"This time still okay?" He motioned toward the screen.

"Yes, it's fine. How's everything in sunny Mexico? I can see you're roughing it up there on your outlook."

"Yep, enjoying this space and the views. I finally got the house livable, so I moved in a few weeks ago. Hold on." He moved to another area which was more shaded. "That's better. So how's things with you? Enjoying England?"

"Yes. It's beautiful down here. Rained a bit, but it was later in the day, so it didn't hamper any exploring." I shared about the trip to the national trust house and my plans for the next day to Greenway.

"Sounds like my kind-of place. I'll have to check it out sometime." He smiled at me through the camera. I suddenly realized how attractive he was with his salt and pepper hair, easy smile, and tanned face. A stray lock of his hair kept falling down in his face adding to his charm. "Here's the reason I'm calling. I'm going to be in London when you are. Let's meet up for dinner some night."

"Oh, you are?" I shifted on the bed and readjusted the pillow behind me. "When?"

"A few weeks from now. I finished book one and decided to make it a series, but with different viewpoints about the war."

When we'd met in Mexico, Perry had explained that he was a historical fiction writer. I'd looked up one of his books and had even read some of it on the plane to the U.K.

He continued, "Since the current one is American focused, the next one will be from an English point-of-view."

"Interesting. When is the first book coming out?"

"Not yet. But if you want to read it and give me some input, I'll send it to you."

He reached up and pushed the stray lock of hair back on his head. "I need a haircut."

"I like it a bit longer like that. It makes you look—"

"What?" He stared at me.

Flustered, I didn't want to say handsome, but instead answered, "Retired."

He leaned back in his chair and guffawed, "Retired?"

I needed to get this conversation back on

course. "Well, I have to say, I may have more insight to give you on the English side now." I told him about my chat with Rodney, about Margaret and Alfred, and also about what had happened to Mrs. Fielding.

Perry's expression turned into a frown and worry lines creased his forehead. "What? Let's hear it. I know you have something on your mind. So spit it out."

"What does that mean?" I shot back.

"I know you. You're thinking there's a mystery to be solved. Right?"

"Well, first, you really don't know me all that well. I mean ... anyway, I just find it curious. That's all."

"You're right. I don't know you that well. So forgive me if I don't want anything bad to happen to you. I thought we were friends."

"We are friends." Why was my voice so squeaky-sounding? I started again, "I'm sorry. I guess I'm tired from today. I didn't mean to snap at you."

"It's okay. No offense taken."

"Once you get to London, you let me know when there's a good time for us to have dinner." His tone had changed and with it a chill had entered our conversation.

"Perry—"

"I need to get off now. Be careful, Vivi." He waved goodbye and the screen went blank.

"Ugh, men!" I signed off and set the computer on the bed. Crossing my arms, I went back over the conversation with him. Yes, he'd been upset with me, but two things stood out. The first was that he cared what happened to me and the second was that he had called me Vivi instead of Viviane. Butterflies again. Maybe there was something more to my feelings than I wanted to admit. But more importantly, what were his feelings? Were we simply friends?

I heard voices on the landing. It sounded like the Caldwells. I sprung from the bed and rushed to my door. Opening it, they both gazed at me in surprise. "Good evening, Viviane. Is everything all right?"

"Yes. I just wanted to say good night to you both as I missed seeing you at dinner."

"We had an errand to run." A look passed between them.

"Well, I didn't mean to intrude on your evening. Good night." I stepped back into my room to shut the doorway.

"Wait!" Edda rushed over. "How is Mrs. Fielding? Did you hear anything?"

"Dianne told us that she has a concussion but should recover."

Edda sighed, "That's a relief. I was so worried about the young woman."

Rodney came over, "Did she say if she fell or—"

Was attacked? The thought rushed into my mind.

"Dianne only told us the basics. But I did find Ivy and ask her if she knew anything else. From what Ivy says, Mrs. Fielding doesn't know what happened. She only remembers looking out the window and the next thing she knew she was being woken up by a medic."

He nodded but said nothing. "Okay, well goodnight, then."

As they entered their room, I heard a soft closing of another door on our landing. Who had been listening in to our conversation? Was it Candace or Holly? They'd come up with me when the game was over. They were going to change rooms in the morning since Charles still needed to retrieve some items. Maybe it had been one of the Carlyles who'd heard voices. I hope we hadn't been too loud. They may have been curious about what Ivy had said about Mrs. Fielding. I locked the door behind me and willed my jumbled thoughts to cease.

I SLEPT WITH THE SOFT PATTER OF RAIN tapping against my window and woke to a bright, sunny day. Making my way downstairs for breakfast, I entered the living room, and spied a lady with soft, blond curls facing the bookcase.

I rushed over. "Mrs. Fielding!"

Daphne turned to face me, and it caught me by surprise. "Oh, Daphne. I, you look like ... I should have realized you weren't her."

A soft smile played on her lips. "Are you going into breakfast?"

I nodded. "Yes. Would you like to join me?"

"That would be lovely." She made a soft wave toward the dining room as Ivy passed us. "Lady Haywood." Ivy did a small dip of a curtsy and went on her way.

Lady? Had I made a faux-pas by calling her Daphne?

She sighed quietly, "I know what you're probably thinking. I married into gentry so I'm still getting used to the titles. I prefer you call me Daphne. Is that all right with you?"

"Yes. Of course."

We entered the dining room where Alfred stood and nodded his head. All this time I thought it was due to a formal English tradition. Though how did he know she had a title? Curious and curiouser. Maybe it was simply that he was of the generation that stood when any lady entered or left the room.

Daphne picked the farthest table away from everyone with a stunning view over the River Dart. We accepted coffee and orange juice while we waited on our meals.

"I know you're curious. You may ask me what you wish."

"You're right. I thought you said that you are living in Buckinghamshire."

"I do at the moment. Right now, there is work being done on Haywood House in Yorkshire. I'm staying with Jocelyn and Edmund until then."

"The Carlyles?"

"Yes. They were friends of my parents who died in a freak accident when I was young. As I'd said before, they became my guardians. Though I lived in a boarding school at the time, they brought me to their house on weekends and holidays."

"I hope this isn't being too forward, but I see you're wearing a ring. Is your husband joining you for your trip?"

A strange look passed over her face. "Sadly, my husband isn't able to join us as he's away."

I wondered if there were some marital issues between the couple, but she certainly wouldn't share that with a stranger.

She regained her composure, "When

Edmund and Jocelyn found out about the work required for the manor, they suggested a holiday." She accepted the plate set before her with a subtle nod.

I thanked the cook as she set my full English breakfast in front of me.

"What about you? Are you married if I may be so bold to ask?"

"It's fine. I'm a widow." I stared at my naked ring finger. I had worn it for over a year but decided to remove it when too many questions brought up painful memories. For a long time, the outline of the ring had remained after I'd removed it. I slipped it beneath the table. "It has been some years for me. That's why I decided to travel. Though my daughter, Renne has given me grief about traveling on my own." I gave a small smile. "Do you have kids?"

"Sadly, Henry and I were never blessed with children. So instead I have horses and dogs." Tears sprung to her eyes. Embarrassed, she quickly dabbed at her eyes with her napkin.

"I'm sorry. I didn't mean to cause you pain."

"It's quite all right. It happens sometimes. Henry was older than I."

I dabbed at my mouth. "I'm sorry. Was?"

She took a breath before answering, "Is. My mind sometimes wanders, and I speak incorrectly."

"I know all about that. And it can happen at some of the most inopportune times too."

She smiled, "Yes, you are correct, and you would understand being older."

Had she just insulted me or been simply making a statement? I chalked it up to a cultural gap versus one of rudeness. I looked around the dining room. The Bancrofts had departed and we were the only ones remaining. "Are you going out with the Carlyles today?"

She shook her head. "No, I am traveling to Greenway for the day and they were going to take a walk on the coastal path. They asked me to go with them, but I declined. I don't care for heights much. But they, Jocelyn especially, have been adamant that I join them before we depart here. She says the views are stunning."

"I'm not a big fan of heights myself, but I plan to do the walk as well. The views do look like something I'd enjoy." I lowered my fork, "I'm also going to Greenway today. Are you taking the ferry?"

"I had planned on taking the train. But if you are going, may I join you on the ferry?"

"Of course. That sounds great. I'd enjoy the company."

"Brilliant."

We finished our meal before walking down to the dock where the boat awaited passenger loading. I got in line while Daphne wandered around a bit before joining me. We handed over our tickets that we'd received from Dianne before leaving and found seats,

Once we were moving on the ferry, we listened as the captain spoke about the history of the river, pointing out sites such as the naval college attended by Prince Philip, and I grinned as we passed the boathouse for Greenway. After docking, Daphne and I strolled up the shaded lane to the formal entrance. I'd purchased a National Trust pass when I'd been at Coleton Fishacre, so I waited while Daphne paid her entrance fee.

Wandering the house and grounds, I enjoyed thinking about Agatha Christie sitting on a chaise, looking out over the bucolic garden while in her mind she plotted someone's murder. We made our way through the trees down into an old forested area that exuded that same Jurassic feeling as the garden at Coleton-Fishacre. Daphne and I strolled along in companionable silence and after a while we found ourselves at the battery overlooking the river.

I couldn't contain myself. "This is so cool."

"Are you cold? Do we need to go back?"

"No. Actually, I meant it's awesome—or as you would probably say—brilliant. When you see something in a photo or on a show, it's one thing.

But to be here, in person, is quite another. This is where she set her book, Dead Man's Folly, I believe."

Daphne laughed. "Sadly, I think you know her work better than I do." She lowered her voice. "Don't speak of it to anyone." She winked and moving away from the short battery wall inquired, "What's the story about?"

"Secrets. I think most mysteries revolve around them. Keeping them, hiding them, and finally uncovering them."

"Yes, I am sure that is correct. I gather the murderer is found out?"

"They always are."

"Not always though."

"You're right. In real life, people have gotten away with murder. But in the books, they always make a mistake or do something that causes their downfall."

"It is cool."

"Yes, cool is right."

Daphne tightened her arms against her chest. "No, this time I meant cool as in chilly."

I laughed, "Oh, yes. You're right. It's pretty shady here and the sun seems to have gone behind the clouds. I wonder if it's going to rain again."

"I hope the Carlyles will be okay up on the

path. I don't think there's much protection from the elements. Ready to leave?"

I agreed and we took the path back toward Greenway where we decided to stop for a bite of lunch before taking in some of the items on offer in the giftshop. I picked up a couple of books while Daphne chose Agatha Christie's book, Dead Man's Folly.

After catching the ferry to Kingswear, we made our way back up to the inn. Entering the lobby, we heard frantic voices downstairs. We took the stairs quickly to the lower floor and found the Carlyles in front of a crackling fire. Edmund was bent over with his head in his hands and a throw blanket over his shoulders. Dianne entered and provided another throw for Mrs. Carlyle which she gratefully accepted.

Daphne rushed into the room. "What's happened?"

Mr. Carlyle raised his head and I spied a nasty red bruise.

She cried out, "Oh, no. Are you all right? What happened?"

He nodded but said nothing.

Daphne helped Mrs. Carlyle to the other chair, rubbing her hands. The woman looked to be in shock. I strode toward the kitchen where I found the cook reading a cookbook. I told her quickly what had happened and requested hot tea for the couple. She replied that she'd make tea for the group and to send Ivy back to assist her.

Returning to the drawing room I spoke to Ivy before turning to the couple. "What happened?"

Jocelyn took in a deep breath before speaking. "We were walking on the coastal path and the weather changed in an instant. The wind was something fierce. I stumbled and Edmund caught me, but he wasn't so lucky." A look passed between her and Edmund.

"Is that right?" I asked Edmund who didn't respond.

"You could have been killed! You shouldn't have gone out there alone—or at all for that matter." Daphne admonished them.

Jocelyn chided Daphne, "We've walked it many times before during our holidays. When the sun is out, we've never had any issues. I think we must have started out too late."

Candace and Holly entered the room. "What's happened?" I joined them over by the doorway and told them the story.

"That's scary," Holly replied.

I turned away from the group and lowered my voice, "Yes, it could have had a very different ending, but besides the knot on his head, they look like they should be okay."

Candace whispered, "Good way to bump someone off. Maybe he'd had enough but changed his mind at the last minute." She made a silly face.

I swiveled to make sure that neither Daphne nor the Carlyles had heard Candace. I thought she was joking. Except the difference in humor between America and England is as broad as the ocean between the two countries and I didn't want anyone to be on bad terms. As an older gentleman, that goose-egg knot on his head was no laughing matter.

Ivy brought in the tea and we all sat in silence as we sipped the warm brew. Dianne had gone back to her office after being assured by Edmund that a trip to the surgery wasn't necessary.

I looked out to the large bank of windows along the back wall. By this time, the rain was coming down in sheets. I was thankful that we'd returned when we did. I heard the front door squeak open and voices. It was Rodney and Edda. For some reason, they'd captured a soft spot in my heart, and I wanted to make sure they weren't soaked to the bone.

"Excuse me, everyone." I sat my cup and saucer down on the mahogany table and met them as they were starting up the next flight of stairs.

"Are you all okay? That weather's nasty out there."

Edda smiled down at me, "Yes, dear. All is well. The driver dropped us at the door, and we had our brollies so just a bit of wet feet."

"We're taking tea in the drawing room." Seriously? Had those words just come out of my mouth? I doubt they ever would again. "Anyway, why don't you join us? I'll get Ivy to bring some more cups and lemon cake."

"That sounds lovely. Rodney, is that all right with you, luv?"

He nodded, "We'll change our shoes and be right down."

"Okay." I put my hand on the banister knob, then turned back to them. "Just so you know, the Carlyles had a nasty incident on the coastal path earlier. He's okay but took a pretty good knock to his head."

Edda reversed course. "Oh no. This is a week of trials."

Rodney was in deep thought. "That's two people who have been attacked."

"No, he wasn't attacked. They were out on the path. And who is the second one?" I realized he meant Mrs. Fielding. "Do you think someone wanted to harm Mrs. Fielding? But why?"

"People that you think are good often are wolves in disguise. Don't forget that dearie." He stared at me over his glasses as if to confirm that I received his dire warning.

"So you're saying that someone hit Catherine. Who would want to do that?"

"Maybe she wasn't the intended victim." He lowered his voice and glanced over his shoulder to the closed doors behind us.

"Then who?"

"Who was in the room before them?" He queried.

"Well, you—" I stopped. "No offense, but neither of you look like Mrs. Fielding." I didn't add that there was also the difference of about forty to fifty-some years.

He responded. "Really? Wait a minute and then come up to our room." Edda sighed, but followed him up the staircase.

"Okay, I'll be up in a minute." I nodded and the pair moved up the staircase past my line of sight. I decided to pop back to the lower level and ask Ivy to make more tea. The mood had lightened, and I could hear chattering as Candace and Holly regaled the group with stories of life growing up in a rural town in America. I found Ivy and then made my way back up to the first floor landing.

The Caldwells' door stood open with Edda's back to me. With the light from the window and her hair up in a towel, she had the same physique as Mrs. Fielding. I gasped.

Rodney appeared from around the corner.

"See, a bit of light, hair covered, a quick glance, and you know the rest."

I didn't know what to say. "But, why? Who?"

"It's rather simple, dear. To keep the deception hidden."

CHAPTER FOUR

"Deception? What are you talking about?" Rodney motioned me into the room and looked out to the landing before closing the door.

Edda shook her head and sighed as she watched him. "Rodney has a theory and he won't leave it."

While I could see his temper flare for a second, he swiftly reverted to his usual calm self. "Justice. That's what I want to see done. Justice."

Edda came over to him. "Rod, luv, the past is the past."

I felt like an intruder as I watched the display of affection between the old, married couple. A lump formed in my throat as I realized that I would never know such a mature love since my husband had died. I cleared my throat and the couple came back to the realization that I was standing there.

Rodney came over to me and took my hands in his. "I don't want to get you involved. As we've already seen, it could be dangerous. I couldn't live with myself if something bad happened and it was my fault."

"But—"

Edda joined him. "No, my dear. He's correct. As much as I believe this is a folly, I can't state it for certain. Now, I am a bit tired. If you don't mind, may I change my response. We won't join you for tea."

"Of course." I took the hint and excused myself from their room. I heard voices on the lower landing and realized it was Charles Fielding. Curious to find out more about his wife was faring, I met him as he was closing the door behind him. He held an overnight bag and Ivy stood nearby. She had the look of a deer caught in the headlights, not knowing whether to stay or run.

"Mr. Fielding, how is your wife?" I realized for the first time that she and I had never really spoken. I couldn't recall her first name in the moment.

"Catherine is fine. A bit groggy still and struggling with headaches, but the doctor feels she'll make a full recovery after the attack."

"Attack?"

"Just a minute." I explained to Ivy that the Caldwells weren't going down for tea after all and she nodded. "I'll let Dianne know." She stole a glance at Charles and then headed to the back staircase toward the kitchen.

Had Charles been going down to the kitchen on his way out when his wife had been attacked or had he been meeting Ivy there? My anger started to rise. Was he one of those men who chased after every young thing? Why meet with Ivy in secret if everything was above board? I started to dislike him immensely. He said something to me, but I hadn't focused on it.

"Sorry, what were you saying? I'm sorry, I'm distracted as I'm worried about Mr. Carlyle."

"Mr. Carlyle? What happened to him? Was he attacked as well?"

"No. It was just he and Mrs. Carlyle on the coastal path. He said the wind had picked up, she had slipped, and while ensuring she was safe, he fell and hit his head."

"That's terrible."

Ivy had returned from downstairs. I moved out of the way as she moved past us and entered the now vacant room with a vacuum cleaner that she had brought up with her.

He waited until she'd entered and shut the

door. "Catherine is now saying she thinks she was attacked. She saw someone in the mirror."

"Who?"

"Her memories are still choppy. All she knows is that she heard something and turned her head. All she saw was the moment before she was hit."

"Was she facing her attacker?"

"No. She saw them in the mirror. A figure all in black." He pushed his hair back. "I think it may be her imagination overreacting."

I nodded. "I guess it would be hard to know what's real and what you imagined."

"Yes. Well, I must be off. Goodbye."

"Goodbye and give my regards to your wife for a speedy recovery."

He exited the front door as I heard Ivy start up the vacuum cleaner. After a quick pop downstairs to make my excuses, I returned to my room and positioned my chair overlooking the river and facing the channel. I'd opened the windows, and a cool breeze came in, lulling me to sleep. I dreamt of mirrors.

After waking from my dreams, I dressed for dinner. Hoping that my attire was formal enough with navy slacks and a cream blouse, I added my favorite travel accessory of a blue and gold polka-dotted scarf. Knowing the need to learn how to travel light, I'd developed my personal capsule wardrobe of a navy and cream base. That way I could easily accessorize with scarves, jewelry or other colored items that didn't take up much suitcase space. With scarves, I could pack quite a few and it easily changed up the outfit to something different. The ability to mix and match the three colors also meant I had a myriad of outfits without the extra weight. Plus, the saying, 'less is more' really applies when you're hauling luggage in a subway or onto a train.

Slipping on a pair of understated navy flats, I glanced at myself in the long Cheval mirror. Each room had been fitted with one of the standing wood mirrors. I made my way over to the window. Turning my head, I looked into the mirror. It was certainly possible that Catherine had seen someone in the mirror. Besides if they'd had something over their face, she may not have been able to tell who it was.

A knock on the door made me jump. "Just a minute."

I opened the door to find Candace and Holly standing there. "Hi, we wanted to see if you'd join us for dinner. We're really interested in this housesitting thing and wondered if you'd tell us more about it."

"Certainly. Be happy to share. Let me grab my key and I'll meet you downstairs."

Holly, who was the opposite of her elder

sister in both size and manner responded, "What would you like to drink? I can let Ivy know."

"A glass of Chardonnay would be nice. Thank you." I closed the door and picked up my small handbag that held my key. From inside, I pulled out my pale pink lipstick and swiped it across my lips. I was locking my door at the same time the Carlyles were leaving their room.

"How are you feeling, Mr. Carlyle?"

"As well as can be expected in the circumstances." He lightly touched the now-prominent bruise on his forehead. "But needs must."

That was a strange remark, but I turned as Jocelyn took his arm in a protective gesture. Or was it more of a warning to stay quiet? Candace had said she'd heard them arguing. Was Jocelyn putting on a show of being nice in front of others?

The woman wore a brooch of diamonds and rubies on her simple gray dress. I'd seen her wear it every evening at dinner. I stepped closer. "Your brooch is beautiful."

"Thank you. It was a gift from Daphne's mother. I treasure it."

May I?" She nodded and I stepped closer where I noticed that one of the rubies was missing. I pointed toward it. "Has this always been like this?"

She glanced down at it and gasped. "Excuse me." She rushed back into her room with

Edmund following. The door shut abruptly. I heard angry, muffled voices from beyond the door.

I stood there a bit confused at what had just happened. Who knows? I shrugged my shoulders. I'm sure that it would be troubling if I'd lost a gem out of a favorite piece of jewelry.

I went down and joined Holly on the long Chesterfield sofa. We enjoyed the time chatting before dinner, but I noticed that Ivy appeared preoccupied. As the announcement was made to move into the dining room, I went over to her and spoke quietly, "Ivy, is everything okay?" She nodded but looked to be on the verge of tears.

I pulled her over to the side, "Are you sure?"

We looked up to see the Carlyles entering. Ivy spotted them. "I have to go help cook." She fled from the room.

The Carlyles approached and I noticed right away that the brooch had been replaced with a different, smaller peacock pin of emeralds, diamonds, and sapphires.

Jocelyn came over to me. "I must apologize for my behavior earlier. I've been having some issues with my brooch's clasp and I saw that it wasn't holding. I've been meaning to have it cleaned and repaired. As you can imagine, it is a cherished piece and the thought of losing it ... well, you can understand my dismay."

Dismay, yes. Outright, panic. No. I nodded, "Yes, I certainly do."

Daphne sidled up to us as she entered the room. "Jocelyn, where is your brooch?"

Jocelyn starred at Daphne before smiling at the women, "I decided to wear this piece instead."

"Oh, I just know how much that trinket means to you and how you treasure it."

Trinket? I could bet that brooch held great value in both sentiment and price.

"Thank you, Daphne. You're such a dear for noticing its importance to me."

"Well, I—" Daphne's response was cut off by Edmund who motioned toward the dining room, "Shall we go in?"

He held out his hand and I realized there were no scratches or bruises. How had such a frail man not scrapped up his hands or arms when he grabbed Jocelyn who was more substantial in weight?

He looked at his hand and then at me. He dropped his hand to clutch both of them behind his back. Turning to Jocelyn, he said, "Ready, darling?"

"You must join us for dinner," Jocelyn smiled at me, but it failed to reach her eyes.

"Thank you for the invitation, but Holly and

Candace had already asked me to join them and I accepted."

"Another time then." She walked over to her table without my response.

Not if I could help it. I don't know what it is about some people, but you just know that you don't click. Her demeanor seemed angry, cold, and dismissive. I liked Daphne and realized I hadn't seen her. "Edmund, where's Daphne?"

"I believe that she decided to sup in her room this evening."

"Thank you." I could almost bet that our conversations during the day had brought up grief that so often came in overwhelming waves. I'd try to check in on her after dinner.

CHAPTER FIVE

I knocked softly on Daphne's door and spoke in a quiet tone, "Lady Haywood, are you up?"

She answered the door and her face bore the evidence of crying. Clutching a handkerchief with a D monogrammed on it in cerulean blue thread, she invited me into her room. I looked around the room and saw that other than a different color palette, it was the same set-up as my own room. However, hers was a larger space and a bay window area held a small settee and two chairs with a table in the middle. "Would you join me for a cup of tea?"

"I don't want to intrude. I just wanted to make sure that you were all right."

She wiped her eyes with the lace-trimmed

hankie. "Yes, I think some of our conversation today brought everything back."

"I'm sorry. I'm not sure what you mean."

She moved over to an electric kettle that beeped. "Please, join me."

I acquiesced and sat down in the chair opposite where she stood. She poured out water and we both chose chamomile from a covered basket. I didn't have that in my room, so I guess the perks of being a Lady did have some advantages.

We sat in silence as our tea steeped. Finally, she spoke, "I'm a widow as well."

"But I thought—"

"My first husband ... He died in a horrible accident, some years back."

"I'm sorry, I had no idea."

She set the bowl back down on the tray, "I must apologize. Stiff upper lip and all that. I failed."

"I'm American. We don't do stiff upper lip. In fact, we're probably more wobbly lips."

She laughed. "Oh, Viviane ... I'm sorry, is it okay if I call you by your Christian name?"

I nodded as I removed the tea bag from my cup and laid it in an adjacent bowl. "Certainly."

"And you must call me Daphne."

I thought we'd gotten all of that name stuff out of the way the other day. Maybe she'd forgotten. "All right." I settled back in my chair and waited.

"How long?" Her eyes met mine.

I knew immediately what she meant. "Grief doesn't keep to a timetable. It doesn't pick appropriate times to hit either. You can feel like you're in a bit of a bubble, correct?"

"Yes. In a bubble. I'll have to remember that." Tears threatened again and she wiped at her eyes.

I clasped my hands in my lap, "I remember thinking that the world was carrying on as if nothing had happened. But everything had happened. My world, as I knew it, was gone."

Daphne laid her hands in her lap. She fiddled with the handkerchief. "This is so refreshing. I have felt that no one could possibly understand. Even the Carlyles, who came as soon as I called them."

"Do they live far from you?"

"Oh, no. They live in Haywood Manor."

I shifted in my seat. "Wait, I thought you said the house was having some remodeling done? I guess I misunderstood."

"Oh, no. That's the hall—where I live. Haywood Manor is a cottage on the estate. It was built before the hall was completed in the seventeen hundreds."

"Seventeen hundreds? I can't imagine living in something that has such a long history."

"It's a big old pile. Or as Herbert called it, a place to spend money."

"I'm sure the upkeep is ridiculous. Oops." I felt the rush of blush creep up my face. "Sorry, we Americans are often blunt in our honesty, too. At least this one is."

"In a way, it's refreshing. Not having to tip-toe around everything in polite and formal conversation."

"But there is something to be said for that politeness. I think, as Americans, we've lost some of that in our daily discussions and interactions with others."

Daphne retrieved the handkerchief from her sweater pocket, and once more dabbed her eyes. "I adored my conversations with Herbert. We talked of so many things. It was the first time I'd felt so happy."

"Sorry, I'm a bit confused. So Herbert was your first husband and your husband now is Henry?"

"Yes, that's correct."

Not to pry. Had you been married long?"

"Five years."

It took me aback. "Oh, I'm so sorry."

She glanced at me over her cup. "I was twenty-five. He was forty. I expected Jocelyn and Edmund to be upset with the match, but they adored Herbert."

Or more likely his money and title. I shoved the unkind thought away. "So the Carlyles lived in the cottage, then?"

"No, the estate caretakers were elderly so I asked my guardians if they would like to live there. They had had some, um, unfortunate circumstances occur, and it would be of a help to them."

My mind whirled. Sounded like some financial problems had hit them, but Daphne wouldn't repeat that in good company. So they had taken care of her and now, she was taking care of them. I gathered that they were in their late fifties or fairly close in age to me.

"I would imagine that it's nice to have them nearby."

"Yes, especially with the ghost."

"Ghost!" I nearly spit out my tea.

"As you can imagine, Haywood Hall has seen a myriad of owners over the ages. Lords, ladies, and others have all lived and died in the hall."

"Have you seen a ghost?"

She shook her head. "No. I don't ... didn't believe in such things. But when Henry would travel up to London, I'd hear strange sounds at night. After a while, I was struggling to sleep. Jocelyn commented one day on my appearance and I explained that I wasn't sleeping well. She suggested that she and Rodney would sleep in the hall when Henry was away. I accepted and after that I had no more sleeping issues."

"Wait, I guess I misunderstood earlier. You said your husband's name was Herbert? I must have misheard."

"No, that's correct. I married Herbert first. My current husband is Henry who is Herbert's father."

Whoa. I tried to hide my shock at this admission, but knew I'd failed miserably.

"I know what you're thinking. Older man, younger woman. But when Herbert died, I leant on Henry for so much. Of course, he was so much older, but his wife had died many years earlier and he was alone." She looked at me over her teacup, "We consoled each other."

"So you married him and became Lady Haywood." I did a quick math equation in my head. He had to be my age or older if his son had been in his forties. That was almost a forty year difference. I couldn't imagine such an age gap.

"Yes, he's such an old dear. He cares for me and I make him laugh."

"I guess if both parties are happy, that's all that matters."

"Quite right." She smiled at me. "So many don't understand. They can be somewhat rude about it. Only of course, not to one's face."

Daphne now had a title and the estate along

with wealth which probably didn't hurt either. Most likely she could not care less what people thought about her. She now had a title, property, and who knows what else to her name.

She set her cup in the saucer. "Why am I bothering you with this silliness? I should be enquiring about you."

"Not much to tell really. My husband died a few years back and I've always wanted to travel more." I shrugged my shoulders. "So, here I am."

"You are brave to travel alone with no companion."

"I don't think of myself as brave. Lots of women travel solo all over the world and in some pretty sketchy places." I glanced at the dregs of my tea. "I should probably say good night. I think I've talked your ear off."

"Did what?"

"Sorry, an American idiom." I rose from my chair. "Let me help you clean this up."

Daphne also rose, "It's fine. Ivy will clear for me."

"Now that you mention Ivy, she didn't seem like herself earlier."

"In what manner?"

"She seemed upset about something." I made my way over to the door, but not before glancing in the mirror. The door to the bathroom was cracked and I spied a black dress hanging up on a hook. Daphne rushed over and shut the door.

Facing me, she responded, "I am unable to speak to her dismay, but I did notice that she was more quiet than usual when she brought up my dinner tray."

"Well, you never know with young people these days."

While she opened the door, I thought, Daphne's not that much older than Ivy. Maybe she has a more mature outlook or views Ivy in a different category than she.

I replied, "Thanks for the tea. Sweet dreams."

After responding with good night, Daphne shut the door behind me. Turning around, I almost ran into Margaret who stood in front of me on the landing.

"Oh, I'm sorry. I didn't see you there."

"One must be careful, mustn't one?"

"Um, yes." I wiped my hands down my slacks.

"May I enquire, is everything all right with Lady Haywood?"

"Yes, she's fine. I wanted to check in on her since she didn't join us for dinner."

"Very well."

I didn't know how to respond to that. Thankfully, the adjacent door opened, and Candace popped her head out of the entry. "Hey there, I thought I heard voices."

Margaret faced me. "Good night." She turned away and I noticed that she was dressed all in black.

"Night." I watched her enter her room and shut the door.

Candace stifled a laugh and stuck out her tongue while producing a crazy expression. She beckoned me over and I walked into the room as Candace closed the door behind me. Holly lay on her bed, reading a book. She looked up and waved, "Hi, ya."

"I couldn't help but overhear Ms. Hoity-Toity out on the landing. Her voice could cut glass."

"I have to agree that she's not the friendliest person I've ever met." I leaned on the wall.

Candace plopped down on her messy bed, tossing a book out of the way. "After she said, 'very well' I kept waiting for her to say, 'you're dismissed.'"

"My thoughts exactly. I'm sure in her eyes we're no-bodies, mere common folk."

Candace made a face. "What's on your mind? I can see the wheels turning."

"Just a strange feeling. I saw Daphne had a black dress hanging in her bathroom and now saw Margaret wearing one. It gives me a weird feeling is all. That's two right in a row."

Holly laughed. "Go open that door." She pointed to the closet. Inside, along with other clothing, hung a black dress. "Everyone has a little black dress. It goes with everything."

"I guess. I don't know. Something about it—"

"Here, have a seat." Candace pulled a chair over and I sat.

"It must surprise her that I've struck up a friendship with Lady Haywood."

Holly set her novel down in her lap. "That's so cool to hear that. I'm having such fun here on this trip. I am sorry about Mrs. Fielding though."

"I spoke with Charles. He said she's doing better, but get this, she thinks she was attacked."

"That's horrible!" Holly sat up straight. "Who would have attacked her, and why?"

"Well," I lowered my voice and leaned toward her, "I heard someone wanted this room pretty badly."

It took her a minute before Holly broke out laughing. "Oh geez. I had to think for a minute."

"That's cause you're not the sharpest tool in the shed, Hol." Candace replied.

Holly stuck out her tongue.

"Nightcap?" Candace ignored her sister.

"Thanks, but no. I've drunk enough tea for the evening. I'm off to bed."

"What are your plans for tomorrow?"

"I haven't really thought about it." Fatigue had settled in.

"Want to join us on a walk along the coastal path? It's supposed to be nice and sunny tomorrow."

"As long as you're not going too early. I plan on sleeping in."

"A lie-in sounds nice." Holly noted.

"Oh, brother." Candace picked up her pillow and threw it at Holly who feigned hurt.

"Okay, see you tomorrow morning." I shut their door behind me and made my way upstairs to my room. Without thinking, I twisted the handle and the door opened. I could have sworn I had locked the door before heading to dinner. Maybe Ivy came in to refresh my tea caddy and forgot to secure the door when she left. Looking around everything seemed to be in place. Except when I looked at the corner mirror, it was shattered.

AFTER A NIGHT OF TOSSING AND TURNING, I rose earlier than normal. So much for sleeping in for a change. I wanted to get with Ivy and let her know about the mirror. I'd picked up as much of the broken glass as I could last night. Despite that, the floor would need a good vacuuming to get rid of any other fragments.

Why would someone have smashed my mirror? Could it have had a crack already or the wind caused it to push backward and break? It could be a fluke, but it left me with a knot in my stomach.

I dressed in layers for the hike on the coastal path. After securely locking my door, I made my way downstairs to the breakfast room. I entered to find the Carlyles and Daphne at a table already eating.

"Good morning!" Daphne chirped.

"Good morning to you too." I addressed the group.

"Join us." Daphne waved her hand toward the vacant chair next to her. "It looks like we may have the same idea."

"Excuse me?"

"Your clothing. Out for a jaunt today?"

I accepted a cup of coffee set in front of me before ordering fruit, yogurt, and granola for breakfast. "Sorry, yes. Candace, Holly, and I are going to walk the coastal path after breakfast."

"So are we." Daphne smiled. Except as I looked over at the Carlyles, I caught them exchanging a glance with each other. No doubt they didn't like the idea of uncouth Americans joining them. Before I'd even finished my thought, Daphne said, "You all should come with us."

"Um, I wouldn't want to intrude." I looked at the Carlyles for their response, but Daphne responded, "Nonsense. We must all go together."

"Yes, of course." Jocelyn replied. Edmund, as usual, remained quiet. His head bore a bandage, but a nasty bruise now colored the side of his face as well.

"How's your head, Mr. Carlyle? I would think you might have a bit of concern going back out on the path."

"I ... well, I'm better. Thank you."

Jocelyn turned to him, "You know, you do look a bit peaked, Edmund. Daphne, would you mind terribly if we stayed in today, darling?"

"Not at all." Daphne faced me. "Will your friends be willing to let me join them?"

"You can ask them yourself. There they are."

Holly and Candace came into the breakfast room with Holly practically bouncing with each step.

"Morning everyone." Candace spoke to the group.

Daphne looked up at the pair, "Good morning."

Holly did a swift clumsy curtsey, "M'lady." I gathered she didn't realize that Americans were under no obligation to bow or curtsey to anyone, even royalty. However, I could tell she was enamored with Lady Haywood and was thrilled to be able to take part in an English tradition.

"I've asked Viviane if I might join you for your walk this morning. Would that be all right with you ladies?"

Holly squealed, then steadied herself, "It would be our honor, Lady Haywood."

Candace, not the one for any of the formal fal-de-ral replied, "Sure."

"Wonderful." She spoke to Holly. "Please call me Daphne."

"Okay. Thank you, Lady Daphne." She bobbed and moved down to a table where the cook stood waiting to take their breakfast orders.

Candace caught my eye and made a face while shaking her head. I stifled a chuckle with my napkin and turned to see Jocelyn and Edmund in whispered conversation. Had they bowed out of the walk because they didn't want to be around us? Edmund didn't look great physically, but he hadn't looked well any time I'd seen him. Maybe Jocelyn was like Margaret in her view of the lower classes and she couldn't stoop to be with us commoners. They didn't have any titles, but maybe they wanted to hang onto Daphne's coat-tails into society.

She addressed us. "If you will excuse us, we'll take our leave now. Enjoy your day, my dear."

Jocelyn rose and Edmund followed her. Once they'd left, I waited until Ivy had removed their dishes before switching my seat to the other side of the table. "That's better. Now I can see you when I talk to you."

"I can see the wheels turning." She motioned toward me.

"Yes. I guess I can't help and be curious about the Carlyles. How did they know your parents?"

Daphne set down her fork. "I'm forgetting where they met, but I think it was during their time at Oxford. The quattour is what they called themselves."

"Quattour? Uh, is that French?"

"It means four in Latin."

"Ah, gotcha." I spooned some of the fruit into the yogurt.

Daphne stared out the window for a moment before continuing. "When my parents had me, the Carlyles became my godparents. They didn't have children as they were enjoying other pursuits. Once my parents died, they took me on as their daughter."

"When did that occur?"

"I was twelve. It was during my time at boarding school. I miss them so much, even to this day."

"I'm very sorry."

"You want to know what happened, but are

too polite to ask, correct?" She arched a perfect brow.

"Guilty." I set my napkin down as Ivy removed my plates.

"Just a moment." Daphne turned to Ivy. "Were you able to take care of my request?"

"Yes. I put it in your room."

"Splendid." She faced me, "Where was I?"

"You were speaking about your parents, but if it's too painful, please don't feel any need to explain."

"They were in a freak accident. They'd gone out rowing on the lake and my mother fell in. She couldn't swim. My father jumped in to save her, but tragically, he also drowned."

"Oh no. How did you find out what happened?"

"The Carlyles told me. They were there when it happened."

CHAPTER SIX

"Oh, that's horrible." I leant back from the table and crossed my legs.

"Yes, the four of them had taken the day to go on the river with a picnic. The Carlyles had gone off rowing their own boat. Sadly, by the time they were able to reach my parents, it was too late."

"Oh no. Was there no one else around?"

Daphne thought for a moment. "I believe the police spoke to an elderly gentleman who'd been walking his dog. But other than that, no one was around to help them."

"I'm surprised that your mother went out on the river if she couldn't swim."

"Father was an excellent swimmer. He'd even been a lifeguard in his youth."

My brow furrowed. "Sorry, I guess I have a

curious mind, but doesn't that seem a bit strange?"

Daphne folded her napkin on the table and laid it to the right of her. She said nothing but looked once more out the window. Had I gone too far with my questions? "I'm sorry. I have no right—"

"Please ... No. I've struggled with this question for years. I even went to Jocelyn and Edmund about it once I left school. I had a clouded memory of it. She explained that the report showed that he had a skull fracture. They think he may have dove in and hit a rock or hit the boat when coming up too quickly."

"How tragic!"

She nodded. "Later I went back to the spot where it happened. It's in a hidden little cove. It's just beautiful there, secluded from the rest of the river. It's probably why no one saw them or were able to render aid."

She took a deep breath. "I'm going to go back to my room before we leave. When do you think we'll be ready to depart?"

I looked past her to where Candace and Holly were finishing up their meal. "Hmm ... fifteen-twenty minutes?"

"Perfect." She rose and the sunlight glinted off of her flaxen hair, giving her the appearance of an angel. "Will you send for me or should I meet you all in the drawing room?"

"Let's meet in their room."

"Lovely." Daphne left and I thought back over our conversation. A secluded spot was awfully convenient if you planned to attack someone. I shook my head. Apparently, I've watched too many unsolved mystery detective shows, and everything held some sinister undertones. Still for some reason, it didn't sit right with me. What I really needed to think about was the here and now, especially concerning the mirror in my room. A mirror doesn't break on its own like that. I motioned to Ivy as she poured coffee for Holly.

"Yes, Ma'am? Did you require something else?"

"No thank you, Ivy." I considered my words carefully. "I've noticed that you haven't seemed yourself the last few days. Is everything okay?"

She glanced over her shoulder and I wondered who she expected to see. "I'm fine. Thank you."

"Okay, that's good to hear. I thought you might be upset about Mrs. Fielding."

Her eyes grew wide and her hands shook. "Why would you say that?"

"Well, I think it's affected all of us."

She steadied herself, "Yes, of course. Will that be all, Ma'am?"

"Just one more thing. Last night when I went up to my room, the door was unlocked. I'm just curious if you went in before I arrived."

Ivy shook her head, "No, Ma'am. I always lock the door."

"I'm sure that you're very conscientious and I'm not accusing you of not locking the door. The reason I'm asking is that my mirror is broken."

Her eyes darted toward the entrance as Margaret and Alfred made their way into the room. "I have to go." She rushed away.

What had just transpired? Ivy was afraid of something—or someone. The Bancrofts sat at the farthest table from the other diners. Only that meant when Rodney and Edda entered, they had no choice but to sit at the next empty table.

Candace and Holly rose from their chairs. I explained that we'd meet in their room before moving over to say good morning to the Caldwells.

"Good morning, Viviane." Rodney looked up as I approached.

"Morning to you all." I motioned with my head. "Beautiful weather today."

He responded louder than usual, "Are you going to visit Slapton Sands?"

"Not today. We're going to hike the coastal path."

"Well, you must see the site of Operation Tiger before you leave."

A flurry of activity startled me as Margaret rose. "Alfred, one is feeling poorly." She hurried from the room leaving Alfred with a stunned look on his face.

As I turned back to Rodney though, he bore a wide smile. What in the world? This place felt like a house of secrets instead of a holiday retreat. I bid the pair goodbye, spoke quickly to Alfred hoping that Margaret would be okay, and then conversed with Dianne about my mirror. After that, I left to gather my things for the hike.

By the time I reached the landing, Holly was chatting amicably with Daphne who leant against their dresser.

Candace stood tapping her foot, impatience on her face.

"Sorry, I'm a bit late."

"Is that a seagull?" Daphne pointed and we all peered out the window. "Ah, too late."

Leaving the room, I explained about the mirror as we made our way outside.

"That's really strange." Candace easily set the lead pace as we headed toward the trailhead. "What do you think happened? Mirrors don't break for no reason."

"I have no idea. I've been trying to figure it out. Plus, Ivy's been acting weird too. Not sure what's up with her."

Holly responded, "I think she's a bit freaked out about what happened to Catherine Fielding. I overheard her talking to Dianne about it."

"Hmm, maybe that's it. I guess its made me a bit jumpy too." I stopped and retied my shoelace.

"Should you require another mirror, you are more than welcome to use mine." Daphne replied.

"I'm fine. I have the one in the bathroom as well as a mirror on the door in there. I'm just stumped on what happened."

While Holly chattered away with the amenable Daphne, Candace and I walked on ahead of them.

Candace lowered her voice, "I don't like this. Do you think someone did it on purpose?"

I stepped off the trail to let another walker pass. "For what reason?"

"I don't know, but don't you think people are a bit weird in this place or is it just me?"

"Well, you are weird ..."

She laughed loudly. "Now I know we're going to be good friends. Continue."

"There have been some strange things that have happened. First, we have all the room changes." I lowered my voice and glanced back to see if Holly and Daphne were listening. Somehow, they had dropped back even farther away from us. "Get this. Rodney thinks that they were the intended target, not Catherine Fielding."

"What do you mean?" Candace picked up the pace and I hurried to keep up with her.

"They'd switched rooms with the Fieldings due to some reservations or something. I can't remember exactly. They even showed me how Edda and Catherine could be mistaken for the same person depending on the lighting."

"Whoa."

"Yes. Whoa. I can't figure out why someone would want to attack them, but there's something going on between the Caldwells—specifically Rodney, and the Bancrofts."

"I've noticed that too. The other day we were talking with them and the Bancrofts joined us. Then Rodney started talking about an operation he'd had, followed by something else, and then about a tiger. I couldn't keep up with all the back and forth. It made no sense to me, but I know that Margaret ended up leaving."

"Hmmm, kind of like this morning." I spoke aloud to myself. "Switching gears. What's your thoughts on the Carlyles?"

"Another strange couple. Though maybe that's just my opinion. Daphne seems nice enough, but they're more snobbish or stand-offish."

"Agreed. They seem a bit overbearing in their relationship with her too in some of the ways they speak to her, but I guess they're simply watching over her like they would their own daughter."

"Um, okay."

"You don't agree." I pulled my water bottle from my small backpack and opened the top to take a sip.

"Something about them strikes me wrong. I feel like they're always keeping an eye on Daphne—overprotective."

"Maybe they're just acting like caring parents?"

I closed the water bottle and returned it to my pack. "Could be. Daphne has really suffered a lot. Her parents died. Then her husband."

"What? I thought he was alive."

"Long story." I glanced back at the pair. "I'll have to tell you later, but boy is it a doozy."

"Okay. So what else? They seem nice enough."

"Daphne hinted that they may have had some financial troubles. But I don't think that's it. I can't put my finger on it. But something's there."

"Understood." I stopped at the sound of Holly yelling for us to wait up.

We took a moment to stop and enjoy the gorgeous scenery. Setting off again, we decided to stop at Brownstone Battery, have a snack, and enjoy the view from that outlook. After our break we pressed on and soon found ourselves walking single file, passing Froward Point on our way toward Old Mill Bay. While the scenery was stunning, I felt a sense of unease in some spots along the path as it would be a long drop to the water and rocks below.

"I wonder where Mr. Carlyle fell?" Holly looked back to where we'd just walked.

"I was just thinking that same thing." I scanned the horizon with my hand over my eyes. "This is beautiful, but a few wrong steps and it could be deadly."

Holly took a step back at my statement, but Candace and Daphne simply nodded. It was a bit of a surprise as I'd thought Daphne had told me she was afraid of heights. Maybe I'd been mistaken.

We pushed on and made our way to the Coleton-Fishacre property. Deciding to have lunch at the café, we strolled the paths and enjoyed taking in the beautiful gardens. I have to admit that when Daphne told me that Haywood Manor looked a lot like this estate, a touch of envy hit. "Well, if you all ever need a house sitter, you know who to call."

"Ooh, me too!" Holly exclaimed.

"When are you going to tell us about the housesitting?" Candace brushed her hair back from her face.

"How about over tea later today?"

Holly jumped into the conversation, wiping her forehead. "As long as I have time for a nap first. I'm knackered."

"Knackered? Really?" Candace sighed.

Holly pouted, "If you went to France, you'd want to speak some French or Spanish if you went to Mexico."

"But they speak English here. We speak English."

"No. We speak American. I think we should try to speak English while we're here." Holly crossed her arms across her chest.

"I give up!" Candace retorted while I glanced over to see Daphne intent on the two sister's exchange. I guess not having brothers or sisters would make the exchange between the pair seem very alien to her.

After a light lunch, we took a different route to complete our circle back to our lodging. I had to agree with the others that a shower and nap would be much welcomed. Back at the inn, we said goodbye, before retreating to our rooms. I found that my damaged mirror had been replaced with another. I showered and laid down on my bed, quickly falling fast asleep where I dreamt of rivers, boats, coastal paths, and screaming.

My mind struggled. Screaming. I bolted upright in my bed. Someone—no it was Holly. Holly was screaming. I threw off the light blanket and ran from the room. Rodney and Edda were on the landing as Edmund rushed out of his room, along with Jocelyn. Daphne appeared dressed in a robe with her hair in a towel. I banged on the sisters' door. Candace came up from behind me and began pounding on the door too. "Holly, it's Can. Open the door!"

We heard a flurry of activity as the door was unbolted and Holly fell into Candace's arms, sobbing. "What is it?" Candace comforted her sister. "Did you have a bad dream?"

Holly sucked in her breath, and spoke, "No ... not if it's real."

Candace held Holly at arm's length. "What are you talking about?"

"It's ... she's dead."

I rushed into the room, but the space was empty. I turned back to see Holly pointing toward the window. Down below on the patio stones lay Ivy.

CHAPTER SEVEN

W e all gathered in the drawing room and hot tea was provided by the cook. Dianne rushed past us, all business, as the different services arrived at the house. We could hear the activity, but none of us could see anything from our view as curtains had been drawn across the windows facing the back. Even though I wanted to find out what was going on, I took the offered cup and sat in silence, sipping at my tea. Poor Ivy.

No one spoke. The only sound was the clock on the mantel ticking away the seconds.

Finally, after what seemed like ages, a policeman came in and each of us were escorted individually to a discreet table in the dining room for questions. I was escorted to a seat across from a man writing notes. After the basics of asking my name and reason for being in England, the detective responded. "My name is Detective Inspector Cameron. Where were you earlier this afternoon, Mrs. Masters?"

"I was napping. We'd all gone on a hike this morning along the coastal path."

"Who was with you at the time?"

"Candace, Holly, Daphne and myself."

He didn't respond but flipped over some other pages. Most likely to see that my story corroborated with that of the others. He made a note on the page, but I had difficulty seeing what he'd written.

"You spoke to Ivy Duncan this morning." He raised his head and stared at me.

"Is that a question or a statement?" I wasn't quite sure what he wanted.

"Did you speak to her?"

"You already know that I did, you just said as much." Yikes, why was I speaking like this? It could be a good way to get into lots of trouble. "I'm sorry. I'm a bit shocked about everything that keeps happening here."

"Elaborate."

"Well, first Mrs. Fielding was hit on the head by someone." He stopped me and riffled through some other papers on the table. Reviewing them, he spoke, "I don't see an attack recorded."

"Mr. Fielding told me as much. I'm not sure

he fully believes his wife, but she said that she'd been attacked."

"She told you that?"

"No, actually Ivy did."

He jotted down a note. "Continue."

I shifted in my chair and looked behind me. Even though we were in another room, I didn't want the others to overhear what I was saying. "There's something going on between the Bancrofts and the Caldwells. It makes sense if Edda was supposed to be the real victim and them changing rooms messed things up. But then why would someone want to hurt Edda? She's a sweetheart. Yet, maybe it was just to get them to leave, because that's exactly what happened after Mrs. Fielding got hurt. And then there's the mirror so it could have happened."

I sat back, satisfied that I'd given some good information. Yet, the expression on the officer's face told a different story.

I may have been rambling aloud, but there was still good information in there.

He gave me that stare again. "You spoke to Ivy. What was it about?"

"The mirror. I just said that. The mirror was broken when I came back into my room. Also, I looked, and Mrs. Fielding could have seen someone in her mirror before she was hit which makes sense. But then they must have known that so ... oh, wow, is that why my mirror was broken?"

"So you spoke to Ivy about your mirror being broken?"

"Don't you see? This means that someone may be trying to kill me. And they got Ivy instead."

The officer sat back and rubbed his forehead. He lifted a page, and looked, "Mrs. Masters, I think that's all my questions for now."

"But, don't you see? She didn't fall. Someone attacked Ivy."

"We will take your statements under advisement."

I huffed. I knew when I was being dismissed and I didn't like it one bit.

I was asked to join the others. Candace came over and beckoned to me to join her outside in the front. Once we moved away from the entrance, she spoke. "That detective's a piece of work, isn't he?"

I nodded. "He didn't even listen to what I had to say." I cocked my head toward the police cruiser. "What are they saying? Did you find anything out while I was talking to him?"

"From what it sounds like, they're saying it's a tragic accident. She must have been carrying the broken mirror to the empty room before it was taken in for repair, stepped back and fell through the window. Three stories can certainly be enough to kill you. You know what they say."

"No, what?"

"It's not the fall that kills you, it's the stop."

My shocked expression registered quickly, "Seriously, Candace? This isn't funny."

"You're right. I don't know why I said such a thing. It's bothered me more than I can say. That poor girl. She didn't deserve that." She buried her face in her hands and sobbed. Wow. I wasn't expecting that response either.

"I'm sorry. I know we're all on edge and you were only trying to lighten the mood."

"No, you're right. It was in bad taste." She accepted the tissues I handed her.

"It makes no sense. Yes, the windows are long and large, but I think it wouldn't be that easy to go through one ..."

"Without a little help you mean?"

"Exactly." She blew her nose.

An officer called us back in and we were allowed to go back up to our rooms. I laid down on the bed before jumping up and striding over to the window. I examined the window and the frame closely. Ivy either had to have been looking out the window or gone head-first. I wondered if they would close off the room where it happened. I paced the floor of my room. From where her body had been it made sense that it was in the corner room on this floor. The same room which had been Candace and Holly's before they'd moved down to the Fieldings' old room. Next to that room was the Caldwells' room, and then mine. Finally, the last room on this floor was the Carlyles.

I went to my desk and pulled out a writing pad and pen. I made a rough sketch of the upper floor plan. Along the back wall I drew the empty room, the Caldwells, and then me. Across the landing was the Carlyles' room. I drew out the floor plan downstairs too. Along the back wall was Daphne's room below the empty room, then Holly and Candace, and on the end the Bancrofts. That meant it would have been Daphne's room that Ivy had fallen from if it had been that floor. I remembered how I'd confused the Bancrofts room for my room when I'd first arrived. Had someone meant to go to Daphne's room and attack her? Instead poor Ivy had been there.

I circled Daphne's name, but she'd been in her room. Though that was only after we had returned. Ivy had at some point come and retrieved the broken mirror from my room. Then replaced it with the mirror from the vacant room. I underlined the word, vacant. Had someone made the mistake I had of getting the rooms mixed up?

Or maybe Ivy had gotten hot and opened the window to get some fresh air. But then what happened? Had she fallen or had someone pushed her? And when had that occurred?

The only reason that Ivy was even discovered was because we all returned, and Holly had looked down on the patio. So there was no telling when Ivy had fallen—or was pushed—to her death. While Edda and Daphne could be mistaken for each other in the right lighting, Ivy was a tall, thin girl with long brown hair that she often wore in a braid.

I sat back and stared at the drawings. I thought back to my broken mirror. Both rooms were on the same floor, but we certainly looked nothing alike. I was shaped differently, at least three inches shorter than Ivy. Besides there was no mistaking my shorter silver hair for her long brunette hair. That meant if it wasn't an accident then someone had meant to kill Ivy. However, it made no sense. Why? She'd been upset the last few days and maybe she had discovered something. I quickly decided against her being so depressed that she'd flung herself from the window. Could Ivy have known something and not realized that she knew?

I tapped the pen on the desk as I considered everything. Something was important, but what was it? Mrs. Fielding! All of it had started with her. I really needed to talk to someone. I went to my computer and fired it up. I shot off a quick email to Perry asking if he was available to chat later today. I sat back, confident that after the scolding he'd give me that he would be able to give me some insights into what was going on here at the inn. Plus, truth be told, I missed him. There, I'd finally said it. Okay, thought it actually. Though after having spent even a short time together in Mexico, I felt like we'd known each other for years.

Walking back over to my window, I glanced down to the patio, but a tent had been set up which hid the area from view. I watched as people in white coveralls with blue latex gloves moved back and forth working the area. At least that meant Ivy's death wasn't being written off as an accident right away. So if it had been murder, who would want to kill Ivy and why? That question was the one that kept returning to my mind.

Poor Ivy. The impact of her death hit me. I sat back down on my bed and emotional exhaustion took over. I laid back on the pillows and my eyes grew heavy. Ivy had to have discovered something was my last thought as I succumbed to sleep.

AFTER BEING INFORMED DINNER WOULD NOT be served that evening, Candace, Holly, and I decided to head to Dartmoor for dinner. Once we ordered our meals of fish and chips with mushy peas, I started to speak to Holly before getting a shake of the head from Candace. I got the hint and took the conversation to a lighter subject.

"Holly, you wanted to know about housesitting."

She looked at me, tears in her eyes. "Ye ... yes." She hiccoughed. "Sorry, I've never—"

"Don't worry. We're all in shock. Ivy was a nice young woman."

Holly wiped her eyes and nose with a paper napkin. "Yes, tragic."

"Come on, Hol, how about a pint?" Candance teased her sister. "Lots of good B vitamins."

"Okay. I'm game."

Candace glanced over at me, "You?"

I looked at my water with lemon. "Sure, why not?"

We flagged the waitress over who took our orders for pints of ale. She bounced off to get our drinks, much happier now than when we'd all chosen waters earlier.

After our ale and meals were delivered, we dove into the food. After we'd all been able to satisfy our hunger, I started. "I learned about housesitting from another lady. She does it full-time, traveling the world for months at a time. I simply wanted to travel so I rented out my house and started applying for sits."

"Did you have any experience?" Holly inquired.

"I'd already been a volunteer at our local animal rescue center, so I had that. Plus, I'd done some pet sitting for neighbors. So those helped as far as having some recommendations. I think it was mainly my age."

"Really? I'd think people would want someone younger."

I took a bite of the grilled halloumi cheese we'd ordered to go with our meals. It went perfectly with the strong ale. Holding up my hand, Holly waited until I'd finished chewing and swallowed. I took a gulp of the ale before answering her question. "It really depends. You have to realize that a lot of older women or couples also travel. If their animals are more used to an older female, then they want someone that is best for their pets. For instance, on a rural homestead, a younger couple may be accepted, because the work is more involved and the area more secluded. So it really depends on what the homeowner is seeking."

Holly dabbed at her mouth. "That makes sense. Do you get paid to sit?"

I shook my head, "No, it's an exchange. You stay in their house, care for the animals and home like it's your own. They get someone to watch their pet and make sure their house is safe while they're away."

"That seems dumb to me. Why go and work for free?" Candace pushed the peas around on her plate, evidently not a fan.

"It's a trade-off. You get to live in a home instead of paying for a hotel which can save you hundreds, if not thousands in cost. It's nice to have a kitchen and you are living in the area you're staying in, so it's less touristy and more of a cultural visit. You get to meet great people and the animals are nice too, especially as a solo traveler. So it's a win, win, for you, the pets, and the homeowner."

"Okay, well that makes sense. Though it still seems like you should get paid." Candace remarked.

I often heard that statement when I shared about housesitting. I answered her, "But that also means that you have to acquire a work visa, pay taxes, etc."

"Ah, good point." She tucked her hair behind her ear.

"Also, it really changes the dynamic from more of a friend coming to stay versus a paid employee. They're very different in expectation and feeling."

"So you made friends in Mexico?"

"Yes, the homeowner, and also I met other house sitters and people who live in the area. You feel like you're a part of the community versus staying in a hotel where you stay in your room and don't really interact with many others."

"How about this? I'll be visiting London for some weeks and won't pay a penny for accommodations."

"Ooh, that does sound good." Holly pointed to Candace and then back at herself. "What about us doing it together? Is that out of the question?"

"I wouldn't see why not. No different than a couple. Plus, it's nice if you have dogs that require more assistance or lots of walking. You can take turns going out or doing it together. Of course, cats are pretty easy as long as they don't have any major needs or health concerns. So you can go out and explore the area, take in a museum, or a show and then simply, return home."

"Candace, I really want to look into this."

"Okay, Hol, we will. But not this minute." Candace set her fork down on her plate.

I smiled at her, "I think you two will really like it. Who knows, we could find ourselves sitting in the same town so we could meet up for dinner."

Holly clapped her hands, "Oh, that sounds like so much fun."

"When we get back to the inn, I'll write down some housesitting platforms so you can sign up. I'll also give you some tips on your profile and how to apply."

"Thanks, Viv."

"You're welcome. I know that it helps my travel budget stretch a lot further."

We finished our meals and declined dessert. On the ferry back, I gazed down at the dark water. What secrets were hidden way below the surface? So many things had happened in the area. I turned to Candace and Holly. "You want to go to Slapton Sands tomorrow?"

CHAPTER EIGHT

In the morning, I struggled to get out of bed. Staring at the ceiling, I thought back to last night when Perry hadn't returned my message. Was he mad at me since our last conversation? I certainly hope not. I wanted—what did I want? Certainly, he had become a friend, but when anything happened my first thought was to share it with him. I hadn't felt that way in a long time. I'd felt something missing for so long and felt that he was the kindred spirit that I needed to fill that void.

I moved the pillow and punched it down to reposition my head. The light streamed into the room and my desire to get up weakened further. I'd left the window cracked last night and a cool breeze ruffled the curtains and made the warmth of my bed even more inviting. I closed my eyes and drifted back to sleep only to be roused by a soft tap on the door.

"Viviane?" It was Daphne.

I swung my feet over the bed and sat on the side. "Just a minute." Glancing at the clock I realized I'd slept hard. It was after ten. Grabbing my jacquard robe from the bottom of the bed, I shoved my fist through one sleeve and then the other. I tied it loosely before unlocking my door.

Daphne rushed into my room and I shut the door behind me. "Is everything okay?" I inquired.

"Yes, I became worried when you didn't come down for breakfast and no one had seen you. I wanted to ensure that you had not taken ill."

I motioned to the chair and sat down on the end of my bed. Yawning, I covered my mouth with my hand before speaking, "I'm fine. I think our hike and all the emotions from yesterday took a lot out of me."

"I too thought of having a lie-in." She sighed. "But unfortunately, the Carlyles want me to go with them hiking on the coastal path. I have no desire to do so since we went yesterday though."

"Come with us." I yawned again. "Sorry, still waking up, it seems."

"Where are you going?"

"There's a memorial to soldiers who were killed in World War Two. From what I gather, they were practicing for the D-Day invasion and someone in the area tipped off the enemy. I think Rodney said that over seven hundred Americans died."

"Oh, that's horrible." Daphne put her delicate, manicured hand to her throat, and I couldn't help noticing the huge emerald surrounded by diamonds she wore.

"Wow. Sorry to gawk, but that's some rock you're wearing."

Daphne looked at it. "Oh, I'd forgotten I had it on. It was my mother's. My father gave it to her when I was born. I treasure it." She stared at me. "Are you all right?"

"Yes. Just something you said. It's reminding me of something, but not sure what."

"It will come to you." She smiled at me from her straight-backed perch on the chair.

"Yes, usually in the middle of the night. So then I'll forget it again. Anyway, why don't you come with us? We're going to rent a car and then do some exploring around the area. Maybe we could gather things for a picnic lunch."

"That sounds lovely." She rose and swept the non-existent wrinkles from her skirt. "Now to share it with Jocelyn and Edmund." She pulled a face.

I laughed. "It can't be all that bad, is it?"

"Now not so much, but as a girl I found that I

ended up going along with Jocelyn's plans more often than not. She would make such a scene, too." She cupped her hand over her mouth. "Oh, I can't believe I said that. I apologize. I must seem so uncouth."

"No, you sound like a woman who knows her own mind."

She rushed over to me, "Viviane, thank you. I appreciate your candor more than you know."

"I've got candor all right. You'll see. When you get older, you realize it's best to be upfront and honest."

"But not hurtful." She looked up shyly at me with a sideways glance, and in a brief second her expression reminded me of a princess who had been tragically cut down in the prime of her life.

"No. Of course not. Truthful, not hurtful."

"May I give you a hug?"

"You might want to wait until I've brushed my teeth and had a shower, but your call."

She laughed and squeezed my hands. "Fair warning. Now, off to the wolves." Daphne opened the door just as the Carlyles were headed up the stairs. Jocelyn stopped just before the top step and Edmund almost ran into her. Daphne quickly put her hands behind her back, fiddling with the ring on her finger so that only the band showed.

Jocelyn approached Daphne, "Darling. You're not dressed for our hike."

"I'm afraid that I must beg off and go with the ladies to Slapton Sands."

A look of fury quickly passed over Jocelyn's face as she glanced at me, but it was instantly replaced with a look of sadness. Wow, the woman was a good actress, that was for sure.

"But, darling," she flew over to Daphne. "Edmund and I have been looking forward to spending this time with you. Our holiday is almost at its end."

"We can still have dinner this evening. But as I've hiked that area yesterday, I don't see a reason to return to it."

"But you must!" Jocelyn cried out before gaining her composure. "I'm sorry, my dear. I am not myself today." She swiveled to face Edmund who'd remained silent. "Edmund, tell her. She must come with us."

I watched as he fought with what to say or do. Jocelyn was a formidable force. "Daphne, please come with us."

Daphne shoved her hands in her pockets before going over to him and kissing him on the cheek. "Thank you for your request. However, I've already accepted Viviane's invitation."

"But you had accepted ours first!" Jocelyn stomped her foot. Was I going to watch a full-blown adult tantrum? I'd never seen her act like this before. Maybe she'd forgotten I was there and had let down her guard.

"You had said something about going today. I don't recall saying I would join you," Daphne replied.

"But you did." Jocelyn's voice had lowered, and her tone was demanding.

However, I had to give it to Daphne who straightened her back and responded, "I'm sorry if I gave the impression that I had accepted. However, I have accepted Viviane's invitation. I will not be changing my mind."

Jocelyn looked past Daphne and if daggers had been real, her stare would have killed me in an instant. She looked back at Daphne, "Well, if you do not wish to accompany us when we have such little time left here, that is your choice. Good day."

Had Jocelyn tried gaslighting? I can see how this would have caused a younger, less strong, Daphne to acquiesce. I waited to see if Jocelyn's words had had their desired effect on Daphne.

"Good day." Daphne turned away and shot me a wink before descending the stairs.

Jocelyn clasped her hands in front of her as if she'd been mortally wounded as Daphne left. The pretense quickly dropped after Daphne was out of sight. Jocelyn then glared at me while

Edmund stood meekly behind her. Under her breath she said, "You have no idea." She spun around and quipped, "Edmund, let's go."

An overwhelming feeling of compassion went out to him as in that moment I seriously considered that he might be an abused spouse. While many think of it with women, far too often, men are victims as well. They are ashamed of it and thus, do not say anything that would damage their pride. With a swift movement, Jocelyn turned toward her room and my eyes met Edmund's. I nodded and smiled. He did the same before following Jocelyn into the room, closing the door behind him.

I glanced over to the door of the empty room where Ivy had taken the broken mirror. Had the event occurred before we'd returned or after? If after, that meant that anyone could have pushed Ivy to her death since everyone had been inside the inn. Of course, someone could have been involved that wasn't staying at the inn but the chances of that were slim. Why would they have come inside? I knew I shouldn't disregard that as an option, but my mind kept repeating that it made no sense. One thing I did know, it wouldn't take a lot of strength—just a push, and then let gravity and momentum take care of the rest. That's when it came to me. She would have screamed. Yet, no one had heard her.

I showered and dressed quickly knowing that the ladies would be waiting on me. Crossing the ferry, we found our rental car and made our way over to the memorial. Of course, tender-hearted Holly dabbed at tears, and even stalwart Candace could be seen wiping her eyes. Later we found a spot along the beach and laid down a blanket where we deposited items from a local grocer of cheese, bread, olives, fruit, and some wine. We chatted about our lives and the day went by in a slow easy manner. We returned to the inn to see a police vehicle sitting outside.

"I wonder what's going on?" Holly inquired.

Candace shrugged her shoulders and strode on ahead, "Well, we're going to find out."

Entering the landing, we heard voices down in the drawing room and we were instructed by a female police officer to join the group there.

Dianne was sitting in a chair by the fireplace, her hands tearing at a used tissue. She raised a blotchy, red face to our entrance but said nothing. The same detective inspector from the other day beckoned us to join the Bancrofts, Carlyles, and Caldwells. Daphne chose a vacant chair while Holly, Candace, and I stood behind the sofa.

Once the DI had our attention, he spoke matter-of-factly. "We are now treating this as a homicide investigation."

"I knew it!" I exclaimed before realizing my

blunder. "Sorry." Oh how I wish I could say 'I told you so.'

He paced the room, making eye contact with each of us. "On the day in question, everyone in this room was at the house during the timeframe that the event is believed to have occurred. Therefore, you are all required to stay here until this preliminary investigation is concluded."

"Whatever are you saying, officer?" Margaret spoke.

"What I'm saying, Ma'am, is that no one is to leave this house."

Holly gasped, "Are we suspects? In a real life murder?" She started shaking and I put my arm around her to steady her nerves.

He faced her but did not respond.

Candace lowered her voice to Holly, "Of course, we are. Someone in this room is a killer."

Eyes darted around the room as if everyone searched to see a clear indication of who could have done the deed.

"One is certainly not a suspect in something so nefarious." Margaret huffed. "Speak up, Alfred."

Alfred looked at her and then to the DI. "Sir, we have nothing to do with the young girl's demise. We didn't even know her other than as our attendant."

"That's what the killer would say." As a

group, everyone fixed their gaze on me. I replied, "Just saying. Obviously, they wouldn't say they did it."

DI Cameron spoke again, "I've retrieved your passports and we will conduct more inquiries from each of you starting tomorrow morning." He looked at Dianne. "Would you like to say a few words?"

She wiped her nose and stood, addressing the group, "Cook is preparing a cold buffet for tonight's dinner. I am dismayed that our guests must endure this horrible tragedy."

I responded, "Ivy deserves justice. However —" I addressed DI Cameron, "Not one of us knew Ivy. Why would any of us want to harm her, much less kill her?"

"Hear. Hear." Rodney spoke up before Edda touched his arm.

"Mrs. Masters, I believe, correct?"

"Yes." I dropped my arm from Holly's shoulders as she appeared more settled now.

"Aren't you the one that said Ivy was most likely murdered, because someone was trying to murder you?"

Gasps filled the room. In unison, Holly and Candace yelped, "What?"

My face grew red. "I ... well I ... yes, I was thinking out loud. Someone had tried to kill Mrs. Fielding."

"Whatever do you mean?" Margaret had risen from her seat. "Mrs. Fielding fell and hit her head. I heard this from the medics directly."

"I think you're hiding something. Maybe it was you!" I retorted.

"Well, I never." She sat back in her chair. "Alfred, say something."

The elderly gentleman spoke, "Detective Inspector, look at this group. I doubt you will find the face of a killer here. Sadly, I believe Ivy had a tragic accident. I had seen her earlier in the morning cleaning the windows. It's possible that she reached out too far and slipped." Alfred rested his case.

"But she didn't scream." I interjected.

"What?" DI Cameron turned to me.

"No one said that they heard her scream. We were all here. If I fell, I would be screaming."

Holly pointed at me. "She's right." She swiveled to the Caldwells, "Did you hear anything?"

They both shook their head.

"What about you?" Jocelyn made a face at being asked a question by Holly.

Instead of responding to Holly, Jocelyn said, "Detective Inspector, I think we should stick to facts, not insinuations. It is possible that she didn't scream or that no one heard her."

I thought about what she'd said. It could be

possible that Ivy hadn't screamed. It could also be possible that she had screamed, and no one had heard her. Yet, it didn't seem likely. Though I'd fallen before and didn't recall screaming as it happened so quickly. Maybe that was the reason —your brain doesn't register it and you don't cry out.

"Were you all out during the morning?" I asked Rodney and Edda, who sat crocheting.

"I'll ask the questions, Mrs. Masters," Detective Inspector Cameron responded.

"How long do you plan on keeping us in this prison?" Jocelyn spoke up.

"Yes, how long does one anticipate this farce to continue? Our holiday is almost to its end." Margaret queried.

Geez, these two sure thought rather highly of themselves.

DI Cameron responded, "At least a few more days until we gather more information from each of you and forensics completes their report. Then those of British citizenry will be able to return home while we must ask that no one else is to leave the country."

"What? We can't stay here forever." Holly yelped, while Candace held her sister's hands.

"Detective, we have a flight scheduled. It's ludicrous to think that we came over from Iowa to murder a young girl who we didn't even know until our arrival."

I nodded at her. "Candace makes a good point. It has to be someone that knew her.".

"We will take your travel plans into consideration once we have reviewed the information. For now, there will be no one who leaves here." DI Cameron bellowed his command.

"Are we finished?" Alfred stood up, and his bearing signaled his previous life as a commanding military officer.

"For now," DI Cameron replied.

"Mrs. Bancroft, is one ready to depart?" He held out his arm which Margaret took, and Alfred escorted her out of the room.

"Lady Haywood, would you care to accompany us upstairs?" Jocelyn's name-dropping had me firmly purse my lips together to keep from saying anything.

"Thank you. I'm fine here. I'll retire in a while." Daphne looked toward the fireplace as if to signal that there would be no more conversation. She had her hands folded in her lap and for the second time that day I noticed that she no longer wore the ring that she had been wearing in the morning.

"Very well, darling." Jocelyn went out and gave Daphne a peck on the cheek before she strode toward the drawing room door with meek,

Edmund, following behind like a puppy would its master.

Edda and Rodney departed next, but not without a look from Rodney that made me think I was being told to stay quiet. About what, I had no idea though. After a quick glance from Edda, I realized she didn't want me to say anything about Rodney's theory.

That left the four of us, Daphne, Holly, Candace, and me with DI Cameron. "You were all out together on the path yesterday, is that correct?"

Our heads bobbed in unison except for Daphne who replied with a polite, yes.

I pounced with curiosity, "Can I ask when you believe Ivy died?"

"You may." He responded before I realized that was the only answer I'd be getting from him.

"I was thinking that the reason none of us heard Ivy scream is that she was killed while we were out of the house."

"Continue."

"That means, that none of us could have done it. We were away for most of the day."

Daphne joined me, "That's right. It had to have been someone who was in the house with her at the time."

"Or someone who came in the house while we were gone." Candace added to our theory.

Holly clutched at a pillow. "I don't like this. You're scaring me."

An officer came in and took DI Cameron aside. We waited as they spoke. He turned back to us, "I have to leave, but be assured that we will have an officer here inside and one outside." He left the room.

I didn't know whether that made me feel safer or more afraid that a killer really walked among us.

"I don't like this. Not at all." Holly moaned and Candace joined her, trying to comfort the frantic woman.

Daphne moved over to Holly, "Let me help you up to your room."

"Thank you, Daphne." The pair left the room. I watched as Candace paced back and forth before dropping into a chair, crossing her long legs.

"I don't like it either. Especially when you think about it."

"What do you mean, Candace?" I sat down on the opposite sofa.

"The screaming thing. If no one heard her, it means that Ivy could have been killed earlier and her body thrown out the window later. That means any one of us could have done it."

CHAPTER NINE

I really wanted to speak to Perry, so I didn't spend much time at dinner. I wasn't the only one that seemed anxious. Gazes darting around the room led me to believe that everyone was sizing up the other guests to see if they fit the profile of a killer. Conversation during the meal was sparse, each of us lost in our own thoughts. Excusing myself to head upstairs, Rodney pulled me aside.

"After you all left with Daphne this morning, Edda and I went back to our room. On the way, we heard the most awful kerfuffle coming from the Carlyles' room."

"Oh, that was probably because Daphne declined to go with them on their walk and came with us instead." I stopped, "Wait, so that means they didn't go out at all today."

"Not that I heard, and we can usually hear doors opening and closing."

"Do you think that one of them had anything to do with Ivy's fall?"

"No. In fact, I know who killed her."

"What!" Who?"

He took my hand to calm me and spoke quietly. "Margaret Bancroft."

I shook my head. "I'm not a fan, but that doesn't even make any sense. What could she possibly have against Ivy?"

"Maybe it wasn't against Ivy. It was the secret Ivy discovered."

"What secret?" A flurry of activity caught my attention and he moved away from me so as to appear that we hadn't been speaking.

The group said goodnight to one another, and I waited to see if Rodney would share anything else, but Edda had arrived.

He placed a kiss on my cheek and whispered, "They deserve justice."

Back up in my room, the day's events were jumbled in my mind. Nothing made sense. I fired up my computer and hit the chat button.

You up? Chat?

Yes. Give me ten. I'll call you.

K

I went to the bathroom where I brushed my hair, washed my face, and applied moisturizer and a swipe of lip gloss. I'd settled back in front of the computer when the connection went through.

"Hi. How are you?" I smiled broadly.

"I'm fine. How about you? Staying out of trouble?"

"I am."

"Why does that not sound sincere?" He sat back in his chair and folded his arms.

"You know about Catherine Fielding. That's still up in the air if it was an accident or someone attacked her. But—"

"Yes?"

"Yesterday, a woman that works for the bed and breakfast died."

He leaned onto the desk, "What happened?"

"From what Detective Inspector Cameron says—"

"Police are involved?"

"She fell from a window which is on the third floor. Someone smashed my mirror ..."

"Oh, it just keeps getting better and better." He crossed his arms again. "You and trouble seem to go together like peas and carrots."

I huffed. "Well, I didn't ask for this. Someone killed that poor girl. I can't leave the country either. That's okay since I've got that housesit coming up in London, but I'm not happy leaving here, not knowing what happened. She was a sweet girl."

"I don't want you involved, but would you feel better if we went through everything together and I gave you my insights?"

I chirped, "Yes!

"Okay. But on one condition. You can only speak to, what's the guy's name—Cameron?"

"Cross my heart that I'll take anything we come up with to him only." I followed up my statement by marking a cross sign in the air over my heart.

"Well, I have my doubts about that, but I know you. You'll be like a dog with a bone about it." He spun his office chair. "Hold on. I'm going to grab something to drink before we start." He returned a minute later holding a glass with ice cubes and a dark liquid in it.

"So she fell—" I jumped in.

"No. Not like that. We start from the very beginning and you tell me everything since you arrived. Often, it's not the things that are in plain view that matter. It's the things you dismiss easily that are where you should focus."

"Now who's been reading too many detective novels?" I laughed.

He said nothing but looked intently at his glass before taking a pull of the drink. I watched as he clenched his jaw and the muscles on his neck tightened. Our eyes met and I spied a focus I'd not seen there before.

Taking a deep breath, I thought back to the day I arrived. It seemed like a long time ago even though it had only been a short while. I shared about meeting all the guests, and Perry instructed me to give a brief synopsis of each one.

I began. "Margaret Bancroft-British upper-crust with an obvious distaste for Americans and her husband, Alfred, who while similar in nature, is more amiable." I explained that they were in their nineties and hadn't been married long.

He raised an eyebrow when I reported this last info but motioned for me to continue.

"Okay, next one." I could see he was writing, and it made me feel that we were a team working together to provide justice for Ivy.

"There's the Caldwells. They are similar in age to the Bancrofts, but they don't put on airs in the same way. They're formal, but I think that's more due to their age and culture. However, they're spending quite a bit of time here. Meaning that they have some money so maybe, upper middle-class. They moved out of the room where the Fieldings' stayed when she was attacked."

"Their names?"

"Catherine and Charles. But they were already gone when Ivy was killed."

"Just taking notes. Now back to the Caldwells." He motioned for me to continue.

"I really like Rodney, but he ..." I shook my head. "He thinks Margaret is the killer."

Perry looked up from his writing, "What makes him say that?"

"I have no idea. He often says some strange things and it's very evident that they don't get on. But today he told me that he believes Ivy found out Margaret's secret."

"Hmmm." He took a swig of the liquor and I gathered it was scotch. He wrote something down and I waited. "Okay, okay." He looked back at me, and replied, "Who else?"

"There's the Carlyles. I don't care for Jocelyn at all. She's always after Daphne to do what she wants. Her poor husband, Edmund just follows her along and doesn't seem to have a backbone. They're Daphne's ... um, well I don't know what they are exactly; they raised her after her parents died."

"Tell me about that and about this Daphne."

"Her name is Lady Daphne Haywood. She's very nice and so different from Jocelyn. Probably did much better by being in boarding school rather than living with them."

He tapped his head with the pen. "And then there's some others?"

"Oh, just Candace and Holly. They don't matter. They're American like us."

Perry quipped, "You like them?"

"Yes, Candace appears gruffer, but she's very protective of her little sister. They're lots of fun and I enjoy being around them."

"Are they divorced, married, widowed?"

"I, um, I don't know. I guess it never came up in conversation."

"What do you know about them?" He sat back and waited.

I searched my mind. Now that I thought about it, they'd not revealed anything about themselves other than the area where they grew up. I guess I didn't know much about them and that caught me off guard for a moment. I paused before responding, "All I know is that they're very nice. I really like them."

He looked at his notes. "You said Candace is very protective of Holly."

"Yes, but I don't mean that she would do something like murder someone. What could Ivy have done to Holly?"

"You said yourself that Ivy may have found out some secret. Maybe it wasn't Margaret's. Maybe it was Holly's instead."

He downed another mouthful.

"That makes no sense. What secret could Holly possibly have?" I grew more exasperated as

I realized my lack of knowledge about the two women. I groaned.

"Never leave out a suspect." I watched Perry closely for some insight into what I felt I was missing.

"What makes you such an expert on the subject?"

He said nothing for a moment, then replied, "We all have secrets. Things that others don't know about us. Every person there has something that they don't want to reveal about themselves. Don't you agree?"

I nodded, realizing he'd never answered my question. I knew he did lots of research for his books as a historical fiction author. Maybe that gave him insight that others might not have.

"Who else should we include?"

"Dianne is the owner, and then there's the cook, but that's it. The Fieldings I've already told you about and they'd left prior to the murder. No new guests have come since then. I'm thinking if anyone had a reservation, that they've been forced to cancel it due to this."

He looked down at his paper and I could see him moving his lips as he counted. "Okay, that's twelve suspects."

"Twelve? No, that's not right. Let's see, the Bancrofts, that's two. The Carlyles, two, Daphne, one. The Caldwells, two. Candace and Holly, another two. I guess we should count Dianne and the cook, two. That's eleven."

"But you're forgetting someone."

I ran the numbers through my head again. Nope, eleven in all. "Wait, you're not including me in that number, are you?"

"You are there, and you could have done it. There's no telling what secrets you hold."

"Ha. Do you really think I have secrets?"

"Oh, yes. Most definitely. It will be fun finding out what they are."

His statement took me aback and I became flustered on what to say in response.

He threw back his head and laughed heartily. "Oh, Vivi, you are such a delight. Haven't you had anyone flirt with you?"

"Of course. It's, well to be honest, it's been a really long time." I felt a lump gather in my throat.

"Vivi, let's stop playing games and dancing around the subject. I think you want to get to know me better and I certainly want to get to know you better. Can we agree on that?"

"Yes." A smiled played on my lips. "Yes, I want to get to know you better."

"Great. So we have to get this resolved so you won't be distracted when we get together for dinner in London."

I cleared my throat. "Okay. Any insights thus far?"

"Talk me through the rooms. I'm going to make a sketch of the blueprint."

"Okay, I'm on the top floor. Next to me are the Caldwells' room. Then there's the empty room where it's believed Ivy fell."

"Didn't you say that Candace and Holly occupied that room when you arrived?"

"Good memory. Yes, they moved to the Fieldings' room after the Fieldings left. Then the last room on that floor is the Carlyles."

"Okay, and the other floor?"

"Hold on. I did the same thing the other day." I went over to my desk and retrieved the sketch. The Bancrofts are in the far right room, then there's Candace and Holly in the middle room where the Fieldings were originally, and the left is where Daphne is staying. Wait. The Caldwells were in the middle room first. Then the Fieldings and finally Candace and Holly."

He stopped and nodded before scribbling on a page. Then he held it up for me to see. It showed the house with three different perspectives. "What is the common denominator here?"

I looked at the drawing. Nothing stood out to me. I shook my head, "I don't see anything."

"Okay, let's change tack. First, Mrs. Fielding either falls or is attacked. Correct?"

"Yes. That's right."

"Then what happens next?"

"Candace and Holly move downstairs to that room."

"Could Ivy have seen Holly attack Mrs. Fielding?"

"Seriously? So you're saying that Holly attacked her because she wanted a different room?"

"When working through a case, you never discount anything."

I shrugged, "I suppose. Yes. I remember Ivy going in with the vacuum cleaner after Charles gathered all the items they'd left."

"Okay and then your mirror was smashed. Why?"

"I don't know. I'm not even sure it was done on purpose."

"Maybe to warn you off."

"Warn me off from what?"

He sat back in his chair, "Why do you use a mirror?"

"To see."

"Exactly. Someone wants you to not be able to tell what you see. It sounds like a warning."

I shivered at his assessment. "I don't know anything though."

"Sometimes it's what you know, that you

don't know, that you know." He winked. "You know?"

"Ugh. We're not getting anywhere."

"Oh, but we are. We've narrowed it down to the most important thing."

"We have? What's that?"

"The room." He stopped and his brow furrowed for a minute. "I'm not crazy about this, but you need to get into that room and search it."

"Search it for what?"

"I don't know. But you will when you find it."

"This is crazy."

He took another sip of his drink. "Yes, it is. You have to be careful with everything you do from here on out. Someone is desperate and it looks like they think you're in the way."

"And there's eleven people who could be the killer."

"No. I said twelve."

"Twelve? Are you still counting me?"

"No. I'm counting Charles Fielding."

CHAPTER TEN

"*C*harles Fielding?"

"Think about it. Maybe they're on the outs. He decides to take her away and in the heat of the moment, hits her over the head. Then he rushes out, so he has an alibi. Ivy finds Mrs. Fielding who survives." He picked up his glass, but it only had a little bit of liquid left. He set it back down.

"Wow. I'd never even considered him."

"His wife recovers and even though she doesn't know who hit her, she doesn't think she simply blacked out either. She thinks that she was attacked and saw the person in the mirror."

"But surely she would recognize her own husband."

"There could be a few mitigating factors. It

was so quick that she only saw a shape versus the actual person or she's blocking out the trauma. If the latter is the case, then she may still be in danger."

"Oh no." My hand flew to my mouth. "What should I do?"

"Get your inn owner to give you Mrs. Fielding's contact information. Then you can either call or go visit her."

"Okay, that's something I can do. But what about the policeman? He said to stay here."

"For the next few days, but then you can leave the inn, just not the country. Isn't that what you said?"

"Yes." I stared off into space, my mind struggling with the idea that the killer could have been Charles Fielding.

"Viviane."

I jerked back to the moment. "Sorry, this has thrown me for a loop. What were you saying?"

"Maybe you can get Candace and Holly to go with you."

"I thought you said that one of them could be the killer?"

"They could be ... Possibly. But I don't see them trying anything out on a trip with you to visit Catherine Fielding."

"Can I tell them what we think?"

"You can share that it's something you've considered. Don't say anything about me though. On the upside, if they had anything to do with any of this, it will cause them to let down their guard with you and to not feel threatened by you."

I shifted my position and stretched. "I'm still not liking the idea of either of them doing something like this."

"People do bad things for strange reasons." He picked up his glass and gulped the last bit of liquid. "Done. Keep me posted."

"I will. Good night."

"Good night, Vivi."

The screen went blank.

I pushed myself up and found a notepad. I needed to get all my thoughts down. Or they would run through my mind all night like a hamster on a wheel running in place but getting nowhere. I made a list of everyone at the inn that day and this time included Charles Fielding.

Had Ivy found something that implicated Charles in the attack on his wife? He knew that Candace and Holly were going to trade rooms, because I'd heard Ivy talking to them about it while I spoke with him on the landing. That was before Ivy went into the room with the vacuum cleaner. What could Ivy have discovered and how would Charles have known about it? He would know that Ivy would be alone in the empty room upstairs. No, wait ... he couldn't know that as he had left. Tomorrow I needed to find out from Dianne where the Fieldings lived and see if Candace and Holly were willing to join me.

I slept fitfully and when the sunlight spilled through the window, I rose early to greet the day. I took my time as I showered and dressed for the morning knowing that we'd have a continental breakfast with a choice of pastries, fruit, yogurt, and cereals. Downstairs, many of the others were already seated at the tables and the conversations were hushed. I strode back toward the kitchen and the small adjacent office where Dianne sat, looking at her computer screen.

I knocked lightly on the door. "Good morning, Dianne. Am I intruding?"

"No, please come in." She shooed the dogs out of the way and motioned for me to sit in a Queen Anne chair positioned next to her mahogany desk. A portrait of a young Princess Elizabeth, now the queen, hung over the desk along with calendars and a layout of the rooms. Each room bore a tag with each of our names on it.

I sat down in the chair and gathered my

thoughts. "I wanted to express my sympathy again, Dianne. I'm so sorry about Ivy."

Tears gathered, but she quickly regained her composure. "It's a tragedy, to be sure."

"Especially after the incident with Mrs. Fielding."

"Catherine Fielding? Why do you say that?" She straightened her back. "Are you wanting a refund?"

"No. no." I waved my hands. "I'm sorry, that wasn't the impression I meant to convey. I was simply remarking about them, that's all."

She sighed and sat back in her chair. "I apologize for my behavior. Mrs. Carlyle asked for a refund, because of everything that's happened and how it's ruined their holiday."

"It's not your fault."

"Maybe not, but she insinuated that it would be unfortunate if our establishment received a reputation for lack of safety and security."

I stiffened up. "That's blackmail."

"I have no choice. But with not being able to take in more guests right now, it's ... I'm sorry. I shouldn't be telling you this. I don't think I've been sleeping well. Again, please forgive me."

"No forgiveness needed. In fact, if anyone needs to ask for forgiveness, it's the Carlyles."

She smiled. "You Americans are always so

forthright in your statements. One would never speak like that as a true Englishman."

"One? Did the Bancrofts also ask for a refund?"

"No. However, if it gets around that I gave a refund to the Carlyles, then I will have to offer it to all the other guests as a courtesy."

"Well, not me. I don't need or want a refund. Anyone asking for one should be ashamed of themselves. You have gone above and beyond in ensuring our stays have been delightful. No one could ever imagine something like this happening, and you have handled it in the best manner possible."

"Thank you. Now, you had something you wished to discuss?"

"Oh, yes. I'd almost forgotten. I've been thinking about Mrs. Fielding. I wonder if you might have an address for them. I'd like to call on her or at least send some flowers." Milo had appeared next to me and I absently petted his head while I spoke.

"That would be nice. I don't normally give out guest addresses, but I'll make an exception for you. I have some of cook's jam I could also send. Let me see, I've got their last bill ready to file." She shuffled through some papers until she came to the needed paper. "Here you go. You can jot down the address from this." She tore a page off of a notepad and handed me a pen.

I looked at the receipt and wrote down the address. Rising, I thanked Dianne and started out of the room before I stopped short.

"Dianne, the receipt for the room."

"Yes?"

"Is that the date you created it?"

"No, that's the day that Mr. Fielding returned to pay the balance. Why do you ask?"

"Just curious. My days are just running together that's all. So that was the same day that Ivy fell?"

Dianne swung her chair toward me, and I noticed a cat in her lap. This was the first time I'd seen one so she must stay away from the dogs. "I'd never thought of that, but yes, he arrived earlier that morning. He'd said that they were missing one of Catherine's scarves and wondered if they'd left it here." Dianne stroked the cat's head and the feline purred loudly.

"So he was here that day?"

"Yes, I think he spoke to Ivy about it, but I had to start on the shopping, so I didn't go with him to talk to her." She set the cat down and I watched as it climbed to a shelf in the corner. Evidently, she must spend a lot of time up on that perch starring down on the dogs.

"So he went upstairs?"

The telephone rang. "Uh ... my apologies, I need to get this."

"No worries. Thanks for this." I waved the paper with the address on it.

As I closed her office door behind me, I stood for a moment letting what she'd told me wash over me. I headed toward the breakfast room, "Well what do you know?"

"I don't know. What do you know?" Candace laughed.

I looked up and saw the pair. "Oh, hello. Good morning."

"What do you have there?" Holly gestured at the paper in my hand.

"I thought I might take some flowers to Mrs. Fielding. Would you two want to go with me?" Now more than ever, I wanted others around and had no desire to find myself alone with Charles Fielding.

"I could certainly use a bit of time away from here. This place is starting to creep me out." Candace surveyed the room as if expecting a ghost to jump out at us.

"Holly, how about you? I just need to get the okay from DI Cameron and then we should be able to take the train."

"Well, Lady Haywood and I have plans tomorrow for tea and a bit of shopping."

Candace wiped her brow, "Whew. Glad I

don't have to tag along for one of your shopping expeditions for once."

"I'd always thought you liked going shopping." Holly huffed and crossed her arms. She was a petite woman, and this only served to make her look like a petulant child.

''No. I don't like shopping. I only go because you don't have anyone else to go with you."

The pair exchanged a look and Holly retorted, "I'll be fine."

"Good."

I wanted to stop this conversation before the two sisters became even more animated. "Great. Sounds like everyone's happy then. I'll speak with DI Cameron and see if it will be okay for us to visit Mrs. Fielding."

"Did I overhear that you're going to visit Mrs. Fielding?" It was Rodney who'd spoken.

"Yes, I thought it would be nice to check in on her and let her know we're thinking about her."

Margaret sniffed loudly and I glanced over to her table, but she had turned away from us. I guess that 'one didn't think about those beneath her.' I stifled a chuckle.

"Are you quite well, my dear?" Edda had joined us, and I jumped as she touched my forearm.

"Yes. Fine, thank you." I guess my face had

given away some emotion as I thought about Margaret's reaction.

"Brilliant. Rodney, luv, are you coming?"

He nodded, but I grabbed at his coat sleeve. He faced me as I spoke to the ladies, "I'll join you in a minute." They nodded and walked over to the table laden with the breakfast buffet goodies.

"Rodney, why do you think Margaret is a killer?"

His face blanched. "Not here. Not now."

"But—"

"Later." He turned away from me and strode out of the room.

Ugh. What's with all the subterfuge?

I joined the ladies and we chatted about mundane things like the weather, the inside of Greenway, the flowers in the gardens, and the trip on the ferry. I noticed that Daphne had not joined the Carlyles. "Has Daphne come down yet?"

Holly spooned sugar into her coffee. "She's taking a day by herself. That's why we're going out tomorrow."

"Okay. Anything on your plans today?"

"Not much. Reading and walking. It will be a nice day for it."

"Did you know that Mr. Fielding came back here on the day that Ivy died?"

Candace stopped her spoon midway, "Whoa.

Do you think he had something to do with her death?"

"I don't know, but it is a strange coincidence."

Holly stirred her coffee. "Agreed. Do you think Ivy attacked Mrs. Fielding and he killed her because of it?"

"What are you talking about?" Candace shook her head. "Really. What are you thinking?"

"You should never discount anything on a case."

They both stared at me.

I laughed, "I think I saw that on a television show."

Holly pointed her spoon at me, "You're so funny, Viviane. I thought for a minute you were serious."

I glanced at Candace, but she said nothing. I may have fooled Holly with my response, but I could tell Candace hadn't believed a word I'd said.

We finished our breakfast and were the last to clear the dining room. The pair left to go walking and I retreated to my bedroom. I needed to figure out what to do if DI Cameron wouldn't allow us to travel to see Mrs. Fielding.

I went down to the office and asked Dianne to use the phone. After placing a call to the detective, I was placed on hold for a considerable time. The cat dropped down from her perch and walked on the desk, watching me to discover that this interloper was doing in her space. Finally, he answered.

"Mrs. Masters, Detective Cameron speaking. How may I help you?"

I explained about wanting to travel to see Mrs. Fielding and take her some flowers.

"Why would you want to do that?"

I shifted the phone, "As a sign of friendship."

"You are friends with Mrs. Fielding?"

I stared at the names of the guests on the wall. "No, that's not what I meant."

"Then what did you mean?"

"A nice gesture is all. It would be me and Candace going. Holly is going to stay here. We'll take the train in the morning and be back by the afternoon."

"I see."

"Does that mean that we have your approval to travel?"

"I'll call you back." The line went dead.

Staring at the phone, I set it back down in the cradle. I looked up to see the cat staring at me with its intense hazel eyes. "I had better come up with a Plan B if he won't let us go. What do you think?"

The cat lifted its paw and began licking it. "I can see you're not going to be much help." I tapped my fingers on the desk. I needed to see

Catherine, but no great idea formed. I had no idea what I could say over the telephone. "Hey, I think your husband may have tried to kill you and Ivy knew it, so he killed her. So watch your back, okay?" I'm thinking that approach might not go over too well.

The phone's ringing startled me. I answered with a cheerful hello and the inn's name.

"Is this Mrs. Masters?"

"Yes."

You can go." He hung up.

"He's not one to mince words." I set the phone back in the cradle. I loved how the inn had retained the feeling of an older, simpler time by keeping many of its things from bygone eras. I'm sure that mobile devices had their place in our modern world, but there was nothing better than to slam the phone's receiver down or to twist your fingers through the cord as you flirted with a boyfriend. I sighed. Everything was so much simpler then and more complicated now. "Well, see you later, Princess." The cat turned away from me as if I had been dismissed from the room.

I went upstairs and knocked on Candace and Holly's door. No answer. They must not be back from their walk yet.

I went up the next set of stairs and as soon as I reached the landing, I could tell my door was open. Rushing in, I saw that the room had been invaded by someone. Drawers had been hastily shut and things were knocked over on the dresser. On my desk lay the paper with the Fieldings address. Except that wasn't what caught my attention. It was the knife that lay next to it.

CHAPTER ELEVEN

First checking to make sure the bathroom was unoccupied; I gathered my courage and opened the door. Empty. I ran back and locked my door. Staring at the knife I wondered what it meant. Was it a warning? A signal to 'cut it out?' Or something even worse.

A knock on my door startled me and I let out a yelp.

"Viviane, it's me Holly."

I unlocked the door and she walked in. "Ah, there it is." She marched over and picked up the knife, waving it at me.

"What are you doing with that knife?" I backed up, looking for an escape.

Holly's eyebrows knit together. "Are you okay? You sure seem jumpy lately."

I pointed at the knife, its blade glinting in the light.

Holly stared at it for a moment as if contemplating what it was. "I asked Dianne if I could borrow a knife as I want to take an apple and cheese with me out on my walk. She must have brought it up to the wrong room."

"But you're not even on this floor." I moved farther away from her.

Holly frowned. "Good point." She took a step toward me and I took one back. "Looks like I'll have to—"

"Confess?" Candace stood in the entrance.

Oh great. I could possibly fight off one of them, but not both of them.

"I'll scream."

"What in the world are you talking about?" Candace shook her head. "I think you're going 'round the bend' Viv." Candace pointed at Holly. "She saw that your door was open and wanted to peek inside your room. She saw that Daphne's room is bigger and wanted to know if yours was any different than the others."

"But what about the knife?"

"I laid it down when I entered." Holly laughed. "You really are a funny woman, Viviane." She moved past me and out to the landing where she hummed as she made her way down the steps.

Candace stared at me. "Really? Holly as a killer? That woman couldn't hurt a fly. I've watched her pick up spiders in a jelly jar and set them outside." She plopped down on the side of the bed. "She does have a big curious streak though. She really shouldn't have come in here, but the door was open."

"But what was she doing on this floor?"

"Edda is going to teach her how to crochet. She came up to talk with her about it and saw your door open."

"You must think I'm an idiot." I leaned up against the door jamb.

"No. I think you're afraid. Like we all are. I've never been in any situation remotely like this. We're all on edge. It's to be expected." She rose. "Now, I'm going to gather my things. What time are you thinking of leaving tomorrow?"

"Fairly early. We'll need to catch the bus to Newton Abbot and from there we can take the train to Bristol Temple Meads."

"That's a ways to go. What if she's not home?"

"I thought of that. I asked Dianne for her email. I sent her a message saying we'd be in town already and wondered if we could stop by for a bit. I also let her know that Dianne wanted to give her some of the jam she liked."

"Smart. Okay. So eight-ish?"

"That works." I closed the door after she left and felt the tension drain away. I needed to keep my wits about me. Not everything was a clue, nor everyone a threat. Despite that I still thought back to my door being open. Someone had definitely been in my room. That was certain. Though had it only been Holly or someone before her and what were they hoping to find? I looked around and everything appeared to be in place.

No, something was missing. What was it?

I stood in the middle of the room, trying to get my mind to give me the insight I was lacking. Finally, I opened my computer to shoot an email to Renne and it took me back to my conversation with Perry. The schematic of the inn. I opened drawers, looked next to my bed, and even checked the trash, but it was nowhere to be found. Someone had taken it. Why? It would certainly be evident that I'd been trying to work things out in my mind. That wouldn't be good to whoever had the most to lose.

I had to be more careful with things from now on and ensure my door was locked before leaving my room unattended.

The next morning Candace and I walked down to catch the bus. We spent our time waiting by taking in the marina, the various boats bobbing in the gray-blue water. It was a quick ride on the bus once it arrived, and we didn't have to wait long to catch our train. We'd both brought books along and spent the time absorbed in the worlds built by the respective authors. The first stop once we arrived at our destination was to find a florist. We decided to splurge and take a taxi. Neither of us had been in one of the black cabs and I wanted to cross it off my bucket list. After acquiring a lovely bunch of flowers in shades of pink, white and yellow, we made our way to the Fieldings' home.

Candace rang the doorbell and Mrs. Fielding answered the door. "Hello. Please come in."

Catherine Fielding was clad in a long corn-flower blue dress that flowed around her. I waited until she had accepted the flowers before entering. We walked past a door to what I'd heard referred to as a snug on British television. Basically the smaller closed off room was for watching television or reading in the evening. We followed Catherine toward the back of the bungalow which was decorated in a simple manner and tidy. Entering what looked to be an extension on the back of the house, a kitchen, dining, and family room overlooked the small back garden accessed through conservatory doors.

"Tea or coffee?"

"Whichever's easier." I replied.

"Coffee, if it's not too much trouble." Candace answered.

"Would you prefer tea, Mrs. Masters?"

"No, coffee works for me too."

She set to making the brew. "Please, have a seat. This will be just a minute." She motioned to the modern table and chairs. Framed pictures covered a nearby piano and I called over my shoulder, "Okay to look?"

"Sure."

The photographs were black and white stills with silver frames. A few showed some current shots of Catherine and Charles as well as some earlier shots of when they were younger. One was a picture of a group of girls in front of a large building with an elderly woman dressed in a suit with a faculty gown. The girls were also dressed formally in checked skirts with white blouses and ties.

Catherine joined me and picked up the photo. "That is my class at the boarding school I attended."

Daphne had also mentioned a boarding school during our conversations. I guess it was fairly standard for those in the upper echelons of society in England.

Now that we were here, how was I going to broach the subject of her husband being a possible killer. So I said what came to mind. "You have a very nice place here."

She pulled cups from a corner cabinet. "Yes, we enjoy it. We haven't lived here long as Charles recently found a job in the area. We moved from Yorkshire a few months back. Our trip to Devon was a much needed escape from work."

Catherine set the cups on a tray and added sugar, milk, and spoons. I popped up from my place. "Here, let me help. We didn't come so you could wait on us. How are you feeling?"

She sat in a nearby chair and Candace poured the coffee that Catherine had prepared. "Better. I still have days where I have horrible headaches, but the nurse attending me says it's to be expected. She assures me it will take some time, but I am healing."

Candace handed me a cup and I could read her unsaid message—get on with it.

"Catherine, I don't know if you've heard, but Ivy was killed not too long after you left."

She cupped her hands around the mug set in front of her and stared at it. "Yes, I did. Dianne informed me about it. She was so young. Tragic."

"Yes, it is."

Candace poured the coffee in our cups and we added milk or sugar as to our desired taste. I waited until the pot had been placed back on the warmer before continuing, "I, we, were wondering. Do you think it had any connection to your attack?"

"Attack?" Who said I was attacked?"

"Charles." I sipped from my cup and waited.

She touched her head. "I don't know. It's all so fuzzy."

"What do you remember?" Candace responded.

"I had come out of the shower. I was putting my hair up in a towel when I ..."

I edged closer, "Go on."

Catherine gazed off into space. "A witch came flying at me. I barely saw her in the mirror. Then a terrible pain." She looked back at us. "The doctor thinks my brain may have been hallucinating. That maybe I'd had a seizure. It's all craziness."

"So a woman, not a man?"

She stared at me. "What makes you say that?"

"You said a witch. That's normally a woman."

Catherine replied, "I'm not sure. They were all in black. Even their face was hidden. It was so quick. I don't remember much of anything."

I could see that her strength was fading fast and I said, "Catherine, I'm sorry to have troubled you. We came to cheer you up, not to cause you more angst." I gathered the cups and took them to the sink for washing up.

The door opened and in walked Charles. "Darling, are you unwell?" He moved over to her and bending down on one knee, held her hands in his. He certainly could put on the charm, but was it all an act for me and Candace?

"Hello." Candace rose and they shook hands. I finished washing out the cups and set them in the strainer before wiping my hands. He walked over to me.

"Hello, again. This is a surprise." We shook hands.

"Yes. We wanted to visit and bring Catherine some flowers as well as some jam from Dianne."

"That's very thoughtful of you, isn't it darling?" He addressed his wife.

"Yes." She whispered and he went back to her.

Placing his arm around her waist to help her stand, he murmured, "Let me help you to the sofa."

With the space between us, I finally got up some courage to speak. "I also didn't know if you had heard the news about Ivy."

He aided Catherine onto the sofa before turning back to me. "Yes, it's terrible."

"You were there that day, I think?" I asked.

"Yes, in fact I saw Ivy."

"You did?" Candace interjected.

Charles gathered a wrap and placed it tenderly over Catherine who had lain her head back and closed her eyes. He took her hands in his and kissed them. Then he motioned for us to follow him to the front.

"Goodbye, Catherine," we said in unison, but she had fallen asleep.

"Thank you both for stopping by. Catherine will be embarrassed that she was unable to entertain you properly, but this has been a hard row for her." He glanced back over his shoulder toward where she slept.

"You said you saw Ivy that day?" I couldn't let this go unanswered.

"Yes. Catherine thought that she'd left a favorite scarf there as she couldn't find it anywhere. But no one had seen it."

Candace folded her arms, "Where was Ivy?"

"Cleaning our room. I asked her about the scarf. But she told me she hadn't seen it and would be on the lookout for it."

"So not up on the third floor?"

"The third floor?"

"Top floor." I corrected.

"What time was that?" Candace butted in.

His puzzled expression grew. "I don't recall. Why are you two asking all these questions?"

"It just seems weird that you came down there when you could have called."

He stepped back. "I'm not sure what you're getting at. I had business in the area, and I needed to finalize our bill, so I stopped by. Again, why this line of questioning?"

"We're just curious as to who could have been there when Ivy—"

"You grockels."

I didn't know what that meant, but it couldn't be good.

"Are you so bored with your lives that you're looking at me as a suspect in Ivy's death?" The lightbulb must have come on at that moment for him. "Are you accusing me of harming my wife? Or Ivy?" He took in several deep breaths and clenched his teeth. "Leave my home. Now. You are no longer welcome here."

"Mr. Fielding, we just want to—"

"Go. Now."

We scooted past him and he slammed the door behind us.

Candace let out a laugh, "Well, I think that went rather well, don't you?"

"Sorry. I guess I'm not great at playing detective."

"It's okay. Plus, now I know he didn't do it."

We began walking down the road toward the main thoroughfare. "What makes you say that?"

"He loves her. If he had done anything, he would have made up all kinds of alibis, but he didn't. No, I don't think he did it."

"If not him, then who?"

A ding sounded on Candace's phone. "It's Holly." She entered in the number and waited for the connection to go through. "Hey, Hol, what's up?" I looked for a café where we could possibly get something to eat. Candace disconnected the call.

"What's up?"

"Holly's upset. Daphne backed out of their shopping trip today. She thought she might still go shopping, but I said I'd come back, and we'd do something together."

"But I thought—" I realized I was pouting as we had seen nothing of Bristol.

"I wanted to explore while we're here too. But I can't leave Holly alone."

"What is it you're not telling me, Candace?"

She hooked her arm through mine. "Let's find a bus or taxi back to the train station. Then I'll tell you."

Tell me what?

Once we were back on the train, Candace waited until we'd accepted some crisps and drinks. I munched on the potato chips, my hunger being only slightly sated. "Spill it. What are you not saying?"

Candace fiddled with the bag of chips. "Holly sometimes has mood swings. They started when she was a young girl. She has a habit of, let's say, collecting, um borrowed, things." She looked up at me and I read between the lines.

"She's a kleptomaniac."

Candace nodded. "That's why I go with her. It's something to do with having someone with her that prevents her from doing it. She manages it very well now that she's gotten older, but it still helps for me or someone to be around. She sees a therapist for it. Has for years." She reached over and touched my hand. "Please, don't think badly of her. I know she would be livid if she knew I'd told you."

I patted her hand before she withdrew it. "I won't say anything."

She sighed, "Sadly, you probably won't have to. Your mannerisms may tell her."

"So she was going through things in my room?"

Candace nodded. "I'm sorry and I know she is too. She didn't take anything though. I asked and she's honest about it."

"Did she take Mrs. Fieldings scarf?" I pulled another chip from the bag.

"I don't know. I can ask her about it. If she did, we can mail it to her. I doubt we'll be accepted in that house anymore."

The train was slowing down, and I watched as people disembarked, going about their day. It's funny how so many of the guests are hiding secrets. Once we started up again, I remarked, "I wonder why Daphne decided not to go with Holly? That doesn't seem like her to break her word."

"I guess we can find out when we see Holly."

"How about we take her out for a late lunch and a drive?"

"That sounds nice. I think she would like that."

Back at the inn, we found Holly in the drawing room. She was focused intently on the crochet work in her hands. As we entered, she jumped up to join us. "Can you believe it? I can't stand that woman."

"I thought you liked Lady Haywood."

"No, not her."

Candace motioned to us, "Let's go up to our room. I need the bathroom and we can discuss where we want to go for lunch."

Upstairs, a young lady was exiting their room. She held a vacuum cleaner in her hand, so it must be the new housekeeper. She smiled brightly at us. "Hello. I've finished in here. Let me know if there's anything else you require."

Holly chirped. "That's Mary. She's the one taking Ivy's place. Nice girl."

We entered the room which showed the track marks on the carpet from the vacuum's path. Candace walked past me and into the bathroom, shutting the door behind her while Holly moved to the chair, still clutching the crochet materials. I stared at the rows on the carpet where the vacuum had moved.

I looked around and noticed where the vacuum cleaner had skirted the bed and dresser. Candace came out of the bathroom, wiping her hands on a towel. "What are you doing?"

"Help me out. Holly, you be Mrs. Fielding." Holly stood and I placed her facing the window. "Can you grab me a bath towel, Candace?"

Candace came in carrying the towel and I handed it to Holly. "Okay, Holly ... Turn and face the window." She did it. "Can you see in the mirror?"

"Just a bit. Should I move?"

"No. Stay where you are." I motioned to Candace. "You walk over to her from the door and pretend to hit her on the head."

Candace strode quickly from the door to where Holly was now pretending to towel off her hair. "Now Holly, you see something in the mirror, so you begin to turn. Candace, you hit her." I watched as they acted out what I thought had happened.

"Yes. That's it." I clapped my hands together. I then looked down at the vacuum tracks.

"What's up?" Candace remarked.

"Quick, help me move this dresser. If I'm right, it's going to show us who tried to kill Mrs. Fielding."

CHAPTER TWELVE

Holly stood off to the side as Candace and I pushed at the heavy wooden dresser. When we were done, Candace cried out, "A dust bunny! We've found our culprit."

I got down on my hands and knees to brush my hands across the carpet. I felt something hard. Picking it up, I looked down at it, shimmering in the light. I stuffed it in my pocket and faced Holly. My thoughts were in a jumble as I tried to make sense of it all and then, like a cloud moving away, it all cleared, and the truth became evident.

"What is it?" Candace remarked.

"I'll tell you in a bit. First though, Holly, why did Daphne change her mind on going shopping?"

"She said that Jocelyn had thrown a real

hissy fit. Well, not her precise words. But that they were coming to the end of their time here and she had promised them that they would do the walk along the coastal path."

"Oh no." I raced over and grabbed Holly who winced at my grasp, "Holly, quick. Find Dianne and get her to call DI Cameron."

"Why?"

"Because I know who killed Ivy. Candace, you coming?"

She bobbed her head and we raced down the stairs.

I started out at a jog but knew that I couldn't keep that pace. Running had never been something I'd enjoyed. I bent over, breathing heavily, my hands on my thighs. "I don't think this is going to work."

"What should we do?" Candace was also breathing heavily.

I told her where I thought the trio were on the path from when Holly said they'd left. "Thankfully, they got a late start or there's no way we can reach them in time."

"What is it? What did you find?" She looked at me.

I pulled out the gemstone. "The other day I noticed Jocelyn's brooch. It was missing one of the stones. I didn't think anything of it, but she flew into a panic. I haven't seen her wear it since."

"Wow, so she—"

I stretched my back. "I don't have time to explain. Please go back and tell DI Cameron to come to the Brownstone Battery area. I think I can keep her occupied until they get there, but they need to come soon, or another person is going to die."

"Okay." She waved at me as she jogged away.

I pushed on, walking as fast as I could, the sound of waves crashing on the rocks below magnified in my imagination. Only once did I stop to catch my breath. Finally, I could see the battery.

Somewhere up ahead a killer waited.

I sped up my pace, searching the area, but there was no sign of the three individuals. The wind was picking up, forming white caps in the water. I had to hurry. I noticed a group of walkers, binoculars in hand. They would never know how they had probably saved a woman's life.

Making my way down the narrow path, I could see Jocelyn with Daphne taking the stairs up to the top of the historical cement platform. Another person arrived and I saw them chatting with them before the pair descended back down. While out of their sight, I raced to join them.

Edmund Carlyle had taken a seat on a nearby boulder. I yelled and waved. "Hello! Hello!"

He shielded his eyes with his hand and returned the wave.

Catching up to him, I caught my breath. "Whew ... that walk is something, isn't it?"

"Yes, I had to stop and rest for a bit."

I scanned the area, but there was no sign of Jocelyn or Daphne. "Mind if I join you all?"

"Not at all." He struggled up from his perch and for the first time, I could see how old and unwell he was. "Maybe you'd like to sit with me here for a bit."

He was stalling for time. I spotted Jocelyn and Daphne in the distance. I yelled, "Hello!" I waved my arms like a maniac. "Do you mind if I run over and join them?"

Our eyes met and he sighed, "Please."

I sprinted up the path, mindful of the drop on my right. I knew one false step could be deadly.

Jocelyn was the first to speak when I caught up to them. Her voice was shrill, "What are you doing here?"

"Our visit with Catherine was cut short so we decided to return early, and all go out to lunch. Candace wasn't feeling well so I decided to take a walk up to the battery and we could meet up for high tea."

Daphne responded, "That's very nice. How is Catherine Fielding?"

I chose my words carefully. "Better. She's still struggling, but I think she'll be okay."

"Does she remember anything of the attack?" Jocelyn inquired.

"Bits and pieces, but the doctor thinks she may have had some vivid hallucinations. So she's not sure if what she saw was real or not."

"What does she think she saw? It might help the police find the killer." Daphne replied.

"Nothing really. Only a dark figure." I laughed. "She said it was a witch."

"Oh well. I guess that's that then." Jocelyn replied.

"Oh, Jocelyn, I found something of yours. I think it's from your brooch." I dug in my pocket and held out my hand. The ruby shone in the light.

"Where did you find that?" She reached out to take it, but I cupped my hand over it.

"In Candace and Holly's room. Of course, it was the Fieldings room before that." I moved closer to her and changed the conversation, "I believe that you're all leaving soon. Is that right?"

Some indistinguishable emotion crossed Jocelyn's face. "We have to get back to our lives." She glanced to Edmund who shuffled to his feet and stared at the ground.

"It's pretty warm right here. Maybe we can move further up toward the platform and it will afford us a little shade." I also hoped it would give the police a bit of cover as they approached.

No one moved. I waved toward the area with my hand. "Daphne, why don't you walk with me?"

Jocelyn caught at Daphne's arm. "Daphne, darling, please walk with me."

Daphne looked between us. "I've never felt so wanted." She laughed.

Edmund had caught up to us and I spied the dark bruise on his head. We all stood in a line and if I couldn't get them to move away from the edge, I was afraid of what she might do.

"Edmund, I see your bruise is healing nicely. Can you tell me what happened again?"

He stole a glance to Jocelyn. "I, fell. Clumsy."

"I don't think so. I think Jocelyn did it."

The woman gasped. "Why would you say such a thing? I love Edmund."

"I know you do. That's why it was so hard."

Daphne stepped back from the path and twisted around, her neck swiveling as she questioned her, "What was hard? Why would you do that?"

"They had to know if it would work." I stated in a quiet voice.

"You don't know!" Jocelyn screamed and tears streamed down her face.

Daphne swiveled back to face me. "Whatever are you talking about? Jocelyn would never hit Edmund."

"She would if he told her to do it."

Jocelyn took a step toward Daphne.

"Don't do it Jocelyn. It's over." I pulled Daphne toward me.

Edmund came over and Jocelyn fell into his arms.

"What's going on?" Daphne her eyes wide looked between the pair.

"They were going to kill you." I stated.

Daphne exploded as she pushed me away, "Are you out of your mind? They would never hurt me."

I took a firm stance and crossed my arms, "When did you go to boarding school, Daphne?"

A puzzled look came over her. "What are you talking about?"

"You said that you were at boarding school when your parents died."

"Yes." Daphne took a step toward me.

"But you didn't go until after your parents died. Isn't that right, Mrs. Carlyle?"

Daphne swiveled back to the couple. "I went to boarding school. Isn't that right?"

Jocelyn didn't respond.

"Didn't I!" Daphne shrilled.

"It wasn't a boarding school. It was a reform school. Am I correct?" I spoke to Jocelyn.

Daphne shook with anger, pointing toward me. "Tell her! Tell her! I was away at boarding school. I wasn't at a reform school." I reached to grab hold of her but lost my grip as Daphne moved toward the Carlyles. They backed up on her approach, clinging to each other before Jocelyn pushed her hand into her pocket. I sprinted over to the trio.

I yelled, "Don't do it Jocelyn! Drop it!" The large rock fell from Jocelyn's hand.

"Why you—" Daphne rushed toward the woman, but I gathered up all my strength and shoved Daphne to the ground. I heard a horrible noise and knew that my arm had been broken.

Through my struggles with Daphne I could hear DI Cameron's voice, "Stop! Police!"

Daphne was hauled off of me, fighting with the policewoman who held her.

DI Cameron spoke, "Mrs. Carlyle, I'm arresting you on suspicion of attempted murder."

I struggled up, cradling my arm. "Detective Inspector, she was only defending herself. But there is a person to arrest for murder. Her!"

I pointed at Daphne, instantly regretting the movement.

"I won't go back there. I won't!" Daphne's head swiveled in search of an escape. She wrangled away from the policewoman and raced toward the cliff.

"No!" Jocelyn screamed.

The policewoman grabbed Daphne before she could throw herself over the edge and along with another officer hustled her back up the path toward the waiting police car.

Jocelyn fell to her knees. "I'm sorry. I'm so sorry."

I knelt by her. "No one can fault you for not being able to take a life."

She wiped her eyes and as I helped her to her feet, she repeated, "I loved her. I tried to love her." Edmund reached out for her. "We tried our best. But we're tired and we're getting old. It has to stop."

"I understand."

He patted me on the shoulder and walked toward the waiting officers.

"Mrs. Masters, it looks like you have some information to share with me."

"Yes, I do."

He looked at me, "But first, let's get you to the surgery."

I nodded as my arm now throbbed with pain. I cradled it against my chest and made my way up to where they were placing Daphne in the police car.

"I'm Lady Haywood. Do you know who I am? I'll have your guts for garters." She screamed like a banshee as the policewoman shut the door and faced away from the car, awaiting further orders. Inside, Daphne banged on the door, but the officer remained unmoved.

Exhaustion overtook me and I wept. Gut-wrenching sobs came from deep inside me and I couldn't stop them. I realized it must be shock and the adrenaline leaving my body. We arrived at the doctor and they gave me a shot to calm me. Luckily, the break wasn't bad. The impact from the fall and subsequent scuffle had caused the pain. I returned back to the inn where I was met by Candace. She helped me up to my room and while I sat on the bed, she ran a hot bath.

"I'm going to be out here, reading. If you need anything, you let me know."

I nodded and she helped me to the bathroom, closing the door behind her. "Don't lock the door. I'd hate to break it down if I don't get a response from you."

"Good to know." I looked at myself in the mirror. My hair was sticking up in every which way and my dirty face already bore the colors of blue, green, and purple bruising. My neck too held the marks of where Daphne had grabbed at it and an abundance of scratches. I gingerly lowered myself in the bath and closed my eyes, allowing the warm water to soothe my sore muscles.

"You okay in there?" A tap on the door brought me back to the present. I guess I'd nodded off. No wonder she hadn't filled the bath up very deep.

"Yes. I'm getting out now."

"Okay. If you need help, just holler." I heard the creak of the chair's springs as Candace returned to her spot.

After dressing in my gown and robe, I exited the bathroom.

"Oh, boy. You are going to have a shiner tomorrow." Candace tapped next to her eye.

"Yes, but I'll never feel prouder for it."

Candace nodded, "And you have every right to do so. You prevented a tragedy in every sense of the word. I put Epsom salt and lavender in the bath so that should help ease some of the tension. I recommend that you have a good rest." She walked to the door.

"This is going to be some cocktail hour tonight."

"You can say that again."

"This is—" She winked at me.

I threw a pillow at her and regretted the motion instantly. She stuck out her tongue before she closed the door behind her after placing the pillow inside. I felt the tears well up and I grabbed another pillow, pulling it close to my chest. Lying on my side, I dozed, and pieces of the puzzle began to move into place. Yet one question still remained unanswered.

CHAPTER THIRTEEN

I dressed in the same outfit I'd worn when I first arrived. However, it took me much longer with the use of only one arm. I had sat back down on the bed to put on my shoes when I heard a tap on the door.

It was Holly. In her hands, she held a beautiful silk scarf. "Here, let me help you. This should take some pressure off of your injured arm."

"Holly, I believe—"

She tied the knot and replied, "I had Dianne call and I tried to give it back to her. I said I'd found it behind the dresser where it must have fallen." A look passed between us, but neither wanted to say anything different.

I touched her on the upper arm and gave a

light squeeze. "It's a good thing you found it, but she doesn't want it?"

"She wants you to have it." Holly bent down and slid my shoes on my feet.

"You better stop that, or I may feel like a proper lady with a personal maid."

She looked at me, "I feel like such an idiot. She had me so fooled."

"Don't. She deceived a lot of people. That's what narcissists do. But her ailment went far beyond that to being a sociopath."

"Here let me guide you, M'lady." Holly took my arm and I welcomed the human crutch. My body was already starting to ache again.

"One must take the assistance offered." I stuck my nose up in the air and we giggled like young schoolgirls.

Down in the drawing room, I was surprised to see that the Fieldings were also present. The Carlyles, now a former shell of themselves, clung to each other while the Bancrofts and Caldwells sat in silence. Candace brought me over a tall glass of water and led me to a vacant chair by the fireplace.

Holly helped me as I lowered myself into the chair and took the water offered. "Thanks, Candace."

"Here, the doctor gave me these to give to

you." She opened a pill jar and I swallowed two pills, grateful for her attention to my care.

DI Cameron arrived from the back with Dianne. She advised us that the cook was working on dinner so was excused from having to be there."

After Dianne found a seat, DI Cameron surveyed the room, "While I would normally take you to the station, this will be much easier. Detective Sergeant Fisker will record and we will create a transcription that you can all sign tomorrow."

"Mrs. Masters, since you seem to have some information on this, we'll start with you. Please give us your statement about the events occurring since you arrived until today's events."

"The day I arrived there had been a lot of room changing. The Caldwells were staying for a few days, but then decided to stay longer. However, that room had already been reserved for the Fieldings and some other guests beyond them. So on the night I arrived, the Caldwells moved upstairs and the Fieldings took possession of the room.

I paused for a moment. "Then Mrs. Fielding was attacked." I looked toward the Caldwells. "At first, Rodney thought that they had been the intended target."

Rodney sprung up from his place. He

pointed at Margaret Bancroft. "You. I knew it was all because of you that those boys died!"

Edda grasped at his arm, "Rodney, please sit down."

"No." He shook turning toward Margaret. "Someone tipped the enemy off and it was you. You said yourself that you lived on Jersey. You wrote a letter and you told them what was going on at the Sands. Isn't that right, Peggy? You're a traitor!"

Alfred shot up from his place. "Sir, I will not have you demeaning my wife that way." He held up his fists like an elderly boxer.

Were we getting ready to watch two elderly gentlemen fight? I stifled a laugh which made the noise louder and everyone turned toward me. I pushed my lips together.

DI Cameron took a step forward. "Gentlemen, sit down."

After the pair had retreated to their respective seats, Cameron turned to Rodney. "That's a serious charge, Mr. Caldwell. Do you have any proof of this?"

"I took pictures. I know that I remember seeing her during that time." He glared at Margaret. "Peggy, walking out with a serviceman."

"One is not called Peggy."

"You were called Peggy then."

Her jaw clenched and she wrung her hands together. Looking around the group she said, "One did nothing of the sort. One would never have talked about the servicemen or what was going on here."

"But you didn't have to." Rodney fumed. "You wrote about it. Loose lips sink ships! You killed those boys. You killed my friend." He broke down, pushing his head in his hands while Edda put her arm across his shoulders.

Her formal façade broke and, in its place, spilled the language of the commoner, "I swear. I did no such thing. I was just a girl, barely a woman." Her whole body shook as she spoke, "I only wrote my parents. It was just a letter. That's all I did."

The room was silent as the realization of what had occurred settled on the group. Margaret jumped up from her seat, "I didn't do it. I didn't. I only wrote my parents. I only wrote my parents." Looking like a trapped animal, she flung herself back down in the seat, and wept.

Alfred looked at DI Cameron. "May we take our leave?"

Cameron nodded. "You may go to your rooms so that Mrs. Bancroft can compose herself. I'll collect your statement later."

The room was silent as the Bancrofts left. Had Margaret unknowingly sealed the fate of those young men? There was no way to know now.

"Us as well, Detective Inspector?" Edda's face was wet with tears as she comforted her husband.

"Yes."

After the elderly couple had left, there was a hushed silence over the room before Candace spoke. "Wow. After all this time. To come face to face with the person you think caused a horrible tragedy."

"Do you think she did cause it?" Holly spoke quietly. "That would be such a heavy burden."

Detective Cameron spoke, "That is not my purview. We will connect with the proper authorities as that is a serious accusation. But my job is to discern information regarding the murder that occurred here." He looked at me. "Mrs. Masters, continue."

I gathered my composure and began again, "Let's see, um, the Fieldings arrived and took over the room. Then Mrs. Fielding was attacked. As I started to say, the Caldwells showed me that from the back and in the right light, it would be easy to mistake Mrs. Fielding for Edda Caldwell. Rodney thought that Margaret had attacked Edda. But I still couldn't figure out why. She didn't know that Rodney suspected her of anything. So it couldn't have been meant to harm

Edda, but Catherine." I turned to Mrs. Fielding. "Then I realized two things. First, you knew Daphne."

"I don't think so." She looked at Charles.

I continued, "But you did. You went to school together. After her parents were killed, and she was out of reform school, she was sent to a boarding school. When I looked at the picture of all your classmates, I thought I recognized you. But it was really Daphne's face that I remembered once I thought about it some more. The evening you arrived, Daphne recognized you and worried about whatever knowledge you had. That's why she fled the room that night. She had to make herself look different. Daphne knew you would put two and two together."

"Two and two together? Whatever do you mean?"

"That she killed her husband."

"What!" The room erupted. All except Jocelyn and Edmund who met my eyes.

"How did you figure that out?" Jocelyn responded.

"It's what you said, Catherine, that got me thinking." I shifted in my seat. "You said that a witch attacked you. All in black."

"Widow's garb." Candace said aloud.

"Yes. I'd seen a black dress in Daphne's room. Except after seeing Margaret wearing one and

Holly showing me hers, I discounted it. But I remembered that something about the dress looked different. A veil had been hooked to the hanger. In fact, if you search her room DI Cameron, you will find a long black dress and veil."

"We have searched her room, and yes, we did find that."

Catherine's surprise was evident, "So, I'm not going crazy."

"Darling," Charles knelt beside her and kissed her hand, "Of course, you're not."

"I must apologize to you, Charles. A friend said that you should never rule anyone out. So that's why we came to you with questions. As we were leaving, that's when I started thinking things over and realized that I thought someone was trying to kill Daphne. Which, well—" I looked at DI Cameron.

"You may speak freely." He turned to Fisker. "Take a smoke." The man left the room.

I turned to Jocelyn, "When did you realize that Daphne planned to kill her husband?"

Edmund squeezed Jocelyn's hand. "It was when she wanted us to move into the house, because of the ghost." He continued. "It wasn't unusual for Henry to be gone up to his club in London, but the times he was away became longer and longer. Not surprising when there's such a large age difference between them. I could see that Daphne was not getting the attention she requires. She's like a sponge. You have to keep feeding it. Constantly.

"Honestly, we thought she'd gotten the help she required." Jocelyn took a tissue offered by Holly.

"But then you also began thinking of her first husband, Herbert."

"What happened to him?" Holly leaned in to hear.

"They attributed his death to food poisoning," Edmund responded.

I leant forward, and asked the pair, "But you had your doubts?"

Jocelyn sighed. "I figured that was a real accident because he was away from the house. But lately, she'd say things in passing about how easy it would be to have an accident with all the construction and remodeling going on. She'd egg Henry on about getting something that required a ladder, but then would stop him with a sarcastic statement about his age or ability. I think she knew how much it hurt him and then he'd try to do it. He almost fell one time, but the groundskeeper kept the ladder from tipping."

"Whoa, this gets crazier and crazier." Candace quipped.

I nodded, "It sure does. But you have no idea. It started much earlier."

"Earlier?" DI Cameron crossed his arms, but Jocelyn spoke to me, "You mean when she killed her parents."

"What?" Holly's eyes were like saucers.

I shifted in my chair, "Correct me if I'm wrong. You'd all gone out on the boats."

Jocelyn nodded her head. She wiped her eyes and nose before speaking. "No, first it was the picnic. We were all sitting around on the blanket, enjoying the day. Pamela had been wearing her emerald ring. I admired it. Laughing, she said, 'Well, it's yours if I die."

She took in a deep breath, "Daphne had thrown a colossal fit. 'She loved that ring. She wanted that ring. It was hers.' I tried to placate her, saying that her mother would live a very long life and it was only meant as a joke. But she was—"

"Insane?" I interjected.

"Yes. Insane with fury. It came on like a light had been switched on. After some time Pamela had calmed her, but I remember to this day the look that passed between her and Robert. I look back now and realized that they were trying so hard to hold it together. She had confessed to me that something was wrong with Daphne and they were looking into therapeutic schools for her. But she didn't want to ruin our day."

Edmund took Jocelyn's hand as her voice quivered, "The three of them set off in their boat. We can't say what happened exactly, but there must have been a struggle. Her mother couldn't swim. She must have been knocked out of the boat. We believe that Robert dove in to save her, but Daphne hit him with the oar. When we made it to them, Daphne was standing in the boat, holding the oar. The ring was never found though."

"Until now." I interjected.

"Until now. That's when I knew we had no choice. She would keep killing without a thought about it. I'd caught a glimpse of it before but thought my mind was playing tricks. Then I saw her showing Pamela's ring to you before she tried to hide it. She was becoming sloppy and that meant she didn't care if we knew. That made it dangerous for us too.

She took a breath, before continuing. The only way for her to have that ring is if she pried it from her mother's finger. All this time, I've given her the benefit of the doubt. It was an accident. She'd simply blocked the trauma from her mind. Maybe Pamela and Robert were fighting, and she had tried to stop them. But when I saw the ring I knew. Plus, I had wondered about Mrs. Fielding's accident. I was so focused on that occurrence; I didn't realize that we had been duped again. I called Lord Haywood but could never reach him. I don't know how she's done it, but I know she's killed him too."

"Wait. I'm confused. Which husband?" Candace interjected.

Jocelyn wrung her hands. "Uh ... I think she's done something to her current husband. He is older, but he's been looking ill the last few times I've seen him. Now we can't reach him. It doesn't sit well."

Edmund cleared his throat, "Jocelyn and I are growing old. We knew that she would continue to kill. Especially when that poor girl was murdered. I don't know what caused Daphne to kill Ivy. Maybe she knew that we were starting to put things together and was trying to get us out of the way." He smiled tenderly at his wife.

"But why kill Ivy?"

"Who knows? Maybe it was seeing the black dress hanging in her room after Mrs. Fielding was attacked. If Mrs. Fielding said it was someone all in black, that would lead suspicion back to her."

"She had to know our rooms would be searched after Ivy died. Isn't it weird that she would bring that dress with her?"

"Not really. She craves attention. It's not

something she wants; it's something she has to have. Like air. When Herbert died, she received so much attention as the grieving widow. But she hadn't fooled us. She doesn't truly understand empathy or grief."

"Oh geez." I said aloud.

"What?" Candace asked.

"I thought she was grieving when all the while she was pumping me for information. But her tears were so real."

"No, my dear. She can make herself cry on a whim. At her parent's funeral, she only cried when someone said how stoic she was for such a young child."

Candace yelped, "Yikes! So she hit Catherine because she thought she knew her. Then killed Ivy because she may have seen a dress?"

"Or it was a whim. You'll have to ask her. Though I doubt she'll ever confess." Jocelyn answered.

"So you knew that Daphne would continue to kill, and you decided that she had to ..." I chose my words carefully, "... Go away. That's why you had Jocelyn hit you, Edmund."

He rubbed his hands together. "I knew Jocelyn wouldn't be able to hit Daphne. I egged her on, 'Hit me. Hit me.' She didn't want to do it and I said we only had a few days left. Finally, I screamed 'Who else has to die?' and she did it."

Edmund looked at DI Cameron. "If you need to arrest someone, arrest me. I don't have long anyway."

Catherine reached over and touched his hand. "Cancer?"

He nodded. "I couldn't leave Jocelyn alone with Daphne. I wouldn't have her harm my darling." Edmund looked at DI Cameron. "I was going to do it. But Jocelyn didn't want me dying with that on my conscience. She said she'd figure out a better way" He gazed at her. "I know you too well, darling. You would have gone too. You deserve happiness for once."

"I have been happy. With you." Jocelyn responded and I realized that all of her anger and meanness had been due to the horrible situation they surrounded them with no escape. I'd read the tension between them all wrong.

Charles spoke, "I think I may know why Ivy was killed."

CHAPTER FOURTEEN

"Why?" We all spoke in unison.

"She was coming down after cleaning Lady Haywood's room. She was holding a brooch and I said something about it. She told me that Lady Haywood had given it to her, asking her to clean it. It was to be a surprise for Jocelyn as she had wanted it cleaned for a long time. Except she didn't want to send it off to the jewelers because she treasured it."

"How did Daphne know that Ivy did that?"

"That would be me. When we first arrived, I'd asked Ivy to help me plan a surprise for Catherine. I'd been given a promotion. I asked if there was a jeweler nearby so I could give her a piece of jewelry as a reminder of this trip. I guess she must have overheard us talking."

"But I heard you two arguing before dinner."

"Unfortunately, I don't know what I did or said, but I must have given Ivy the wrong impression after she helped me. Ivy mistook my being nice for something more." Charles shrugged. "She told me she'd broken up with her boyfriend and I gave her a hug and kissed the top of her head. She was just a kid. I meant it like I would a daughter."

Dianne spoke for the first time, "Ivy was emotional after the breakup. And things would go missing and then turn up. She finally admitted that she was worried about being sacked. She was especially afraid of the Bancrofts as Margaret had given her a good dressing down one day."

She continued, "Ivy used to work in a jewelry shop and knew how to clean antique jewelry. She must have told Lady Haywood, or she found out. I know that when she came downstairs, she said that Lady Haywood claimed she'd pay her 150 quid to do it. Ivy couldn't say no to that. Poor girl. Ivy didn't deserve that." She pulled a tissue from her pocket.

I spoke my thoughts aloud. "Ivy must have cleaned the brooch and was going to put it back in your room," I looked at Jocelyn. "But when I saw it the brooch was damaged. Missing this." I pulled the jewel from a pocket. "Sorry, forgot about it in the moment."

Jocelyn took it. "It was a message. She knew

how much I treasured that brooch."

"Ah, now I get it."

"Get what?" Candace reacted. "What am I missing?"

"By taking the stone out of the brooch she was signaling that something Jocelyn treasured could be taken from her. And what better place to get rid of it when she was leaning up against the dresser the day she was in your room."

Candace picked up the thread, "I bet Daphne lured her into the vacant room next door, took the brooch and then, hmm ... she didn't push Ivy out of the window then. And we know that Ivy didn't scream."

DI Cameron's voice was stern, "She was drugged. She was unconscious when she went out the window. We actually believe she fell from Daphne's room, not the empty room."

"That makes sense. We just assumed she'd fallen from the top story. Daphne meets Ivy to have tea and drugs her. She takes one of the jewels out from the brooch and puts it in the Fieldings' room. But it gets pushed under the dresser. She knows that Jocelyn loves that brooch and will be upset that she's lost one of the jewels. Now that you've said how she destroys things you love; it makes sense that she wanted to upset you by first taking it away, making you think you'd lost it, and then removing one of the stones.

"I'd noticed Jocelyn wearing the brooch every evening, it would be of conversation or at least speculation. Then when the jewel was found, Jocelyn would come under suspicion taking any such focus off of Daphne in case someone had seen her in the Fielding's room."

"She's calculating all right." Candace interjected.

Holly plopped down on the sofa, "But she seemed so nice."

Catherine interjected, "I didn't realize that I knew her until you mentioned the picture. She had been at school with me and was like that in school too. Nice to your face, but cold when your back was turned. Girls left school many times due to pranks and no one could figure who had done them. But I knew in my heart." Catherine looked at Jocelyn. "That's why I remembered you. When you came to collect her. She must have known that sooner or later I would start putting things together."

"I think it's probably more of her dreams when she was a girl about marrying into wealth and being the lady of the manor."

Catherine bolted erect. "Oh! That's why she had to get rid of me."

"Why?" We asked in unison.

"It just came to me when you said that. Of course, we all talked about marrying a prince or some such nonsense. But she said that she wanted the castle, the title, and all of it, but she'd ditch the prince." She looked around at all of us. "I never thought she meant kill them, but now it's so clear what she implied." She hugged herself. "She could have killed me. Poor Ivy probably saved me from being her target." Rocking, she made a fist in front of her mouth, stifling the pain as tears wound down her cheeks.

"You're lucky—though I'm sure it doesn't feel like it—that she only wanted you gone instead of dead. I think Ivy just came in handy for her." I took a sip of the now tepid water.

"Yes, I guess I can say that."

I looked up to DI Cameron. "Has Daphne made any statements? When will she to go trial?"

"I am afraid that Lady Haywood is undergoing a psychopathy test to determine if she has DSPD."

Holly questioned, "What's that?"

"Dangerous severe personality disorder."

I stretched and groaned as my body responded. "So no trial?"

"If they determine that she is a danger to others, they will most likely recommend indefinite detention somewhere like Rampton Secure Hospital."

Jocelyn could be heard crying. "We failed her."

I leant closer, "You didn't fail her. You tried to help her. That's all anyone could do."

Edmund watched as the officer returned to the room. "Are we going to be charged, DI Cameron?"

"I don't see what charge I could conceive." He turned to the officer, "We'll pick this back up tomorrow."

I clutched at the chair, the aches in my body growing. I needed to stand up for a bit. "Are we free to go?"

He didn't answer as the sound of his phone ringing interrupted. He turned away and lowering his voice, spoke into the receiver. When he completed the call, he turned back to us. "They've just discovered Lord Haywood's body."

Jocelyn cried out. "We failed him too. Edmund, we failed everyone."

Detective Inspector Cameron left without another word with the officer following.

The room was quiet except for the sniffling from Jocelyn. We each sat in a stunned state of silence. I felt a nudge. Milo laid his head on my leg, looking up at me with those sad, brown eyes. I bent over and whispered to him, "Thank you. You knew exactly what I needed."

Dianne had left a few minutes earlier, returning to let us know that dinner would be served shortly. We went into the dining room where all the tables had been moved together to create one long table.

The cook had outdone herself, but none of us were partaking. Finally, Charles pushed back his chair and stood. "To Ivy." We repeated his sentiment and toasted with our wine.

Edmund stood, "To the most loving, caring, beautiful woman in the world. My wife." He took her hand.

"To Jocelyn." We drank. The warmth of the drink soothed my tattered soul.

Jocelyn stood next to him and gave him a peck on the cheek. She picked up her glass. She raised it. "To Viviane. Who stopped me from making a fatal error that I would have regretted for the rest of my life."

A male voice sang, "For she's a jolly good fella ..." It was Rodney with Edda by his side. They must have come in while we were toasting. Everyone joined in and finished with "And so say all of us." They toasted me. "To Viviane."

Tears sprang to my eyes. "Thank you. You're very kind."

Rodney and Edda joined us at the table, but the Bancrofts stayed away. Only as we were eating dessert did we hear voices on the landing. Dianne entered the dining room to let us know that the Bancrofts had left.

After all this time, there was probably no way

to prove Margaret's guilt or innocence. Rodney had said what he thought to be true. All that any of us knew was that she had sent a letter to her parents, but whether it held the damning information, no one could say. Even though Margaret had looked down on all of us as not quite up to par, I felt sorry for her. If she had made that grievous error, she would have to live with that for the rest of her life.

Later I had made it up to my room helped by Candace and Holly. Candace handed me the pills. "You should be okay taking these, but you might want to wait until you absolutely need them since you had wine at dinner."

I nodded and we hugged gingerly. Holly reached up and gave me an air kiss on the cheek. "Sweet dreams."

I knew I needed to call my daughter and Perry too, but the exhaustion of the day lay heavy on me. For now, I needed to sleep.

The next morning I shot Renne an email. I didn't want her to see me like this, so I made the email light and said I'd contact her in a few days. I hoped that by then the swelling and bruises would be less noticeable. Perry was another story. I'd already committed to another call with him and I knew he would know something was up if I begged off. I'd borrowed some pancake makeup from Jocelyn and together with Candace's help had tried to conceal as much of the bruising as possible.

Taking a deep breath, I connected to Perry. As soon as the video went live, he said, "What's happened to you?"

So much for old-fashioned makeup.

"I fell on the coastal pathway."

"So you put on makeup? I know concealment when I see it, Vivi. What really happened?"

I broke down sobbing. The emotions of the last days pouring out.

"Listen, here's what I want you to do. You cry it out. I'm your shoulder even though my real one isn't there quite yet."

"I'll be fine. I'm just sore, that's all."

"I need to turn off my video, but I'll keep talking to you. Go and splash some cold water on your face. It will make you feel better."

"Okay." I left the computer and, in the bathroom, took a tissue and wiped off all the heavy, worthless makeup. I splashed my face with water with my one good hand, then lightly toweled it off.

"Vivi, are you there?"

I hurried back out to the room, but Perry's voice sounded muffled.

"Vivi?" There was a tap on the door.

I opened it to find Perry clutching a bouquet of flowers.

"Perry!" I flung myself into his arms and sobbed on his chest.

Finally, I pulled back and to my dismay saw that his shirt was wet with the remnants of my makeup and my tears. "Oh no. I'm so sorry."

"It's okay. I have another shirt downstairs in my backpack."

"What?"

"There's no way I'm letting you travel to London by yourself. After our conversation, I became more worried about what was happening here. I decided to come earlier and meet you here. By the looks of you, it's a good thing I did."

He handed me the flowers, "Besides, I told you I was coming to the UK for research on my next book."

"What's it about?"

"A plucky widow who doesn't know how to stay out of trouble."

"Ha. Ha."

"You could have been killed, Vivi."

A shiver passed over me. What he said was true. I'd never known a real life murderer or at least not to my knowledge. I moved away and sank down on the bed. "I could have died."

"This isn't some fun vacation thing. It's dangerous. This is twice now that you've gotten yourself mixed up in something criminal."

"Well, truth be told, I was kind of drug into

the first occurrence. However, you're right about this one. Still if I hadn't of stopped things, who knows what would have happened?"

My heart went out to Jocelyn and Edmund who had carried such a terrible burden for so long.

Perry sat next to me on the unmade bed. "You wouldn't do anything differently though, would you?"

"Probably not."

He took my hand and kissed it. "I know."

"So you're going with me to London?"

"To London."

The next book in the Viviane's Adventures Mysteries series is **Larceny in London.** To get on the list for upcoming releases, opportunities for free books, and other fun giveaways, sign up at www.vikkiwalton.com

I'd love to hear from you. You can contact me at vikki@vikkiwalton.com and I will do my best to respond to any correspondence within a few days.

AUTHOR'S NOTE

I hope that you enjoyed reading Deception in Devon. If so, I'd appreciate if you'd leave me a review on your favorite reader and/or retailer site. I appreciate those reviews and you taking the time to write them. So, thank you!

Now, I realized that you may wonder how I came up with the idea for this book, so let me give you a glimpse into how my mind works. Years ago, I went on a trip to England and along the way met many nice people. Ask any writer and you'll find that the way someone looks, the way they speak, even a particular mannerism goes into a file in the author mind for later perusal in case it can be used in a story. From there the fruit of our imagination connects with that of the real world. So we might include a real place, such as Devon, or a real event such as the one that occurred in World War Two but everything else is "made up." People are often composites of people who have come into our lives, sometimes for a while and other times simply in passing. But they combine to create the characters that come to life in our books. They are the people that you'd love to know in person or hate to meet. But let's start with our main character, Viviane Masters.

You might wonder, how did Viviane present herself to me? Well, for a while I've been thinking about a series around a global house and pet sitter. I began this journey as a sitter myself some years back and thought it would be a good way to instill some armchair travel within a cozy mystery. When I was asked to participate in writing a short story for a cozy mystery collection: Mystery Follows Her, Viviane introduced herself to me. It wasn't hard as we had some similar traits but like all of my characters, some have a piece of my personality but they're not me. They're a personality that comes to life in my mind's eye and they decide who and what they become.

So that said, let me give you some insights into Viviane's first adventure mystery, Deception in Devon. Some years back, I accepted a housesit in Bracknell, United Kingdom. It was my first trip to the country and as I'm a huge Agatha Christie fan I knew I wanted to visit her home,

Greenway. Going there had been on my list for a very long time and I highly recommend it for any of her readers or even anyone who has watched the Poirot series. I took the train down to Kingswear where I booked into a local bed and breakfast. I believe that the place where something occurs is also a character in the story and so the house itself becomes a main fixture in this story as well.

Earlier in my life, I had set out to be an architect but switched to interior design as I realized I loved the visualization of how a place should look. Maybe that's why Anne in my Backyard Farming series lives in a fixer-upper Victorian in Colorado, while Christie is setting out on building a cordwood silo-style home in my Taylor Texas series. Now with Viviane traveling the world, I get to indulge my love of different homes and places along with the need to travel more in the future.

Opps—a bit of a rabbit trail there. Anyway, from that trip to England, I was able to experience some things that I have added into the story to bring in a s sense of place. While the story is strictly made up, I enjoyed adding in remembrances of the place. It's a great way to travel to Devon without leaving home and if you can go there at some point, even better.

Of course, none of these characters in the book are real. So what IS real?

The house (bed and breakfast) where I stayed. The main living areas in the book are what people in the United States would call the basement level, while the ground floor is where the entrance is located, and then the second floor (first floor). Confused? Just know that if you were looking at it from the back you would see three stories. Unfortunately, I'd been informed the owners were selling it when I visited and when I looked for it again as a reminder of the area, I didn't see it listed. So they may have closed down the bed and breakfast or sold it. It was a delightful place and I'm glad I was able to visit it when I did. I'm sure there are other delightful places to stay in the area.

The use of *one* as you or I. People of a certain generation and class in the United Kingdom still use 'one' in place of you or I. During my trip, I met a lovely couple (unlike the snooty Bancroft's) and loved hearing her use that term. There were in their late eighties and had only been married a few years which was a fun discovery, so I included that in the story as well.

Viviane's goof at opening the wrong door. The floors looked so similar. And when you know your door is the second off the stairs, it's easy to forget that you must go up two flights of stairs. Yes, I did this and was very embarrassed at my goof! That's one thing that you get to do as an author is let your characters make some of your dumb mistakes. Viviane probably wouldn't have done that if not for me, she's much more polished.

The drawing room. All the guests meet there before dinner in the nearby conservatory. If you're a fan of traditional mysteries and everyone gathered together, you can imagine my delight at this tradition when I arrived at the place I would be staying. While we do gather before meals in places in the USA, this was a different experience and one I'll treasure forever. It also helped me to determine how many people should be staying at the inn while the events are taking place. Alas, there were no other Americans there during my stay so Candace and Holly were created to provide the much needed sidekicks for Viviane's Adventure in Devon.

Coleton Fishacre was something I found out about while staying at the house. During my visit to the estate, I fell in love with the house and its gardens. You can walk down a long pathway and the foliage is so lush, you expect to hear a dinosaur stomping through the leaves. There is a gate at the end which connects you to the coastal path. While there, I met a couple while having lunch. Strangely enough, her son was in my town of Colorado Springs in the United States while I was there. The saying that it's a small world is really true.

The story told by Rodney. I met an older gentleman and his wife (not Rodney) while staying at the house and over dinner he told me about being sent down on the train from London. He also shared about the submarine coming up next to him in the river. In the story, Rodney tells that story to Viviane over dinner. It was also the first (and most likely) the last, I'll ever be called a Yank. Because these stories are literally dying off, I included it in my story. This gentleman also clued me in to the sad history of the Americans who'd died around the point. This tragic event was something I had never heard of before. I'm sure that there are many stories that we'll never know. I think it's because people just consider them part of their life story. That said, I urge you to tell your family and friends your stories. Or even better, write them down. Future generations will want to hear what you have to say about life.

Slapton Sands and Operation Tiger are both real. You can visit them today. It could be that someone tipped the enemy off or that they were discovered through other methods. But it was—and remains a tragedy of that war. If you're interested in military history, it might be something to explore.

What is NOT real?

Of course, the characters in the story are all made up. Other than Viviane, Perry was introduced in the short story, *Hijinks in Ajijic*. The story which is set in Mexico is another place where I've house and pet sit. It's a very laid-back place and I completed my story, *Cordial Killing*, while there. For me travel is a great time to get out and explore, but with housesitting, it also acts as a sort of writers retreat. I don't have to worry about the chores that need to be done and the other many items on my to-do list. There are limited interruptions and it's a time to think, plan, and write.

Printed in Great Britain
by Amazon